Misadventures in London

Misadventures in London

and Elsewhere

Paddy Jacaranda

2011

Fastnet Books
227 Donnelly Street
Armidale New South Wales 2350
Australia

www.fastnetbooks.net

publishing@fastnetbooks.net

First published in 2011.

National Library of Australia
Cataloguing-in-Publication entry:

Jacaranda, Paddy.

Misadventures in London and elsewhere

ISBN: 9780987171207 (pbk.)

A823.4

Cover design by Paul Adams

St Augustine's, Burra

No one ever arrived in London less well prepared than I was. Few turned up there angrier than me. Not that I was entitled to be that angry, but I was.

My family are Catholics and I grew up going to Catholic schools. I'm imaginative and easily influenced, and in my junior primary years I fancied myself a very spiritual young boy. About halfway through primary school I started to turn my attention to social matters and politics. This was in the mid-sixties so my preoccupations were not so odd as they might seem today, but I was conceptual and had a tendency to be extreme.

The whole thing might have sprung from a question that was asked and answered one day in church when I was in third or fourth class. The question had to do with the poor. It might have been to do with the poor in a specific crisis in South America or some other place a long way away, but the answer has had me pondering.

There we were, us twenty-something children, all about eight or nine years old, sitting in the church and a teacher (it might have been a special catechism teacher) asked us what we should do for these far off poor people. It was a multiple-choice question and the option I went for was to give them some money. This turned out to be wrong. The correct answer, apparently, was to pray for them.

There are two things that need to be mentioned here. The first is that I was used to topping my little class at St Augustine's in everything academic (except spelling) and I was not accustomed to being told I was wrong. So I found it very difficult to accept the different answer. But, even accepting the possibility that I could be wrong, I struggled with the answer and still struggle with it today. It seemed to me that it was a cop out. Rather than sending these poor people something they could use, and which would deprive the giver of something he or she could use, we were being told just to pray for them. To my mind, this was a cheap and easy option, and not necessarily the right one.

Whether this moment prompted my political questionings or they just happened to be rousing at that time I do not know. I began, however, to think about politics and social justice.

Initially I didn't have any special allegiance, just a blossoming wonder. I was aware of my family's religion and I somehow formed the vague impression that people like my parents were supposed to vote for the Democratic Labor Party, or DLP as it was called. I asked my mum who she voted for and she said that she voted for the Labor Party. When I asked her why, she said that she voted for the ALP because our local MP was Mr O'Shaughnessy who attended the same church that we did.

From then on my mind wandered around and about political issues; I was sort of trapped in the orbit of the political. This I believe was at the end of my year in fourth class. The Vietnam War was still going on and my preoccupation with economics and social justice led me deeper and deeper into the left of politics. I don't know if I had heard of the Yippies but that was the direction I was headed. I recall a debate with my father one day while I was still in primary school. Exasperated, he eventually burst out: 'All right, be a bloody communist then'. I wasn't a communist, but I was certainly sympathetic to the Viet Cong without being sure why.

This was a strange place to arrive at mentally because I, like many others of the same vintage who first heard about the war on radio, initially thought that the troops in Vietnam were fighting gorillas and only later came to realise that they were not fighting with bands of apes but with other groups of people who were labelled as 'guerrillas'.

My experience at high school, which was largely an unhappy one, entrenched my fascination with left wing politics. I was sent to a conservative school where the emphasis was on sport. I liked sport and was good at it but I was also obviously different. I was neither a nerd nor a jock, but being in more or less constant contact with the physical kids meant that there was more friction and opportunities for confrontation. I was bullied but fought back and, because I was often in fights, I was frequently disciplined. At the start of my third year of high school I had been given more strokes of the cane than anyone else in the school, and the brothers were pretty liberal with its use. I recall having a fight with another boy who relentlessly abused me, and was then given six strokes of the cane on each hand for fighting. That was excessive.

My difficult high school years hardened the edge of my social dissatisfaction. I was very aware that my dad worked on the mine but the fathers of most of my school peers were farmers, pastoralists or urban professionals. They were very conservative and so, I found, were their sons. The Australian Labor Prime Minister, Gough Whitlam, was sacked just as I was finishing school. A history teacher and one of my classmates spent the day of the dismissal in a broom closet listening to the radio. I attended classes but broom-closeted in the breaks. For the next week or so, which were my last in high school, every morning began with an informal political debate in which I was one of only three students who opposed the sacking of the Labor government.

I don't want to give the wrong impression about my political interest during my school years. It was not as if I only read left wing political texts. Far from it! I did read a little of that but I read a great number of novels and many of these were science fiction. And, I should point out that one of the earliest political influences was *Mad* magazine.

After I finished school I found myself back in my home town working on the mine. It was a very well paid job but I wasn't happy. Where others saw security and wealth, I saw the callousness and ruthless of an industry that had been built on the deaths and broken bodies of countless workers. Foolishly, after the first year on the mine, when I should have left and gone to study law at the University of Adelaide, which is what I wanted to do at the time, I went instead to the Gold Coast where at 18 years of age I hit the bars.

This was the true onset of a kind of daze. Unknowingly, I was already in a position to take up the opportunities I sought but I lacked the confidence to leave town and to make my own way through the studies I desired. It took me the better part of three years to leave the mine and it was a mistake to take so long. I coped through that time by drinking more and more beer and smoking more and more cannabis, which I associated with rebelliousness, but eventually I had to go.

Fortunately, because the job was so well paid, and I was only paying a small rent at home, I had several thousand dollars to play with when I left the mine, my family's home and the town.

My girlfriend, Narelle, had moved to Adelaide and I travelled down there before going to Canberra. A few weeks later I went back to Adelaide and moved in with Narelle. I was really lost and the pot and alcohol weren't helping. I needed to do something but I didn't know what.

Narelle was sharing a house with Eliza and Peter. I didn't have much to do with Eliza but I was very close to Peter who was, and I believe is, a real softie. When I met him, he was a charming and erudite university drop out who was, as he put it, 'driving desks and herding files for the old diggers'. Peter had been studying philosophy in Melbourne but was disillusioned by the superficial exercises in categorisation and gave the game away, never to return. In Adelaide he was working for the Department of Veterans Affairs.

Peter had a photocopy of Guy Debord's *The Society of the Spectacle*. I consumed it. I read it in a day and it seemed to make perfect sense. I was reading a book every day or so at that time so that was no big deal but *The Society of the Spectacle* had a tremendous impact on my addled young mind. The book appeared to offer something I was craving. It seemed to cut through and connect me with the world beyond my immediate surroundings.

The Society of the Spectacle was the main text of a French political movement that was known as Situationism and which had peaked in May 1968. Looking back I have no clear picture of what exactly *The Society of the Spectacle* was saying or trying to articulate. I suppose what I took from the book was that our's was a time of alienation where reality had receded from view and we were lost in an artificial realm, an 'immense accumulation of spectacles', conjured by the market economy; or something like that. In any case, the book struck a chord with my agitated disaffection and seemed to validate it in some way.

Not long after I read Debord's book, either Peter or I tracked down another Situationist text: *The Revolution of Everyday Life*. This didn't have as powerful an impact but it should have had none whatsoever because it was, and is, a complete load of crap, but I didn't know that at the time.

Even before I had left Burra, my friend Larry and I had been talking about going to India. In fact we had already decided to go there when Larry had an accident in his brother's uninsured car. That was the end of Larry's travels for a while and it killed off our dream of a joint expedition to the subcontinent.

One day a few months later when I was wondering aimlessly around Adelaide I looked in the window of a travel agent where there was a deal on a flight to Bombay. I was full of marijuana and had plenty of money so I was primed to make a huge rash decision. When I spoke to the agent it transpired that the very same flight that would take me to Bombay went on to London and it actually cost less to go to London. You could sit in the same seat and it would cost you more to get out sooner. That was ridiculous, I thought, and bought a one-way ticket to London.

While the purchase was capricious and had been promoted by the foibles of international flight retailing, at the back of my mind was a political agenda. I supposed that if there was to be great political change that it would take place in a great city, like London. One of the first things I did when I got there was to visit a bookshop in Camden Town that, I was told, would have copies of these Situationist books. They had a copy of *The Society of the Spectacle* and I purchased it.

I've got to say that the book did not have that powerful message that I imagined it had when I first read it. Freshness, naivety and a green tobacco would explain the difference. Even so, I remained very influenced by its ideas, which I took to mean that the most spontaneous, situational, political acts were the most legitimate and productive.

Earls Court

I made no preparation at all for my trip to London except that I got a passport and a visa, bought some travellers cheques, and arranged for almost all of my money to be transferred to an account that could be accessed from a branch of the Commonwealth Bank in The Strand. I had not looked at a single brochure and I hadn't organised any accommodation. I knew almost nothing about London and I certainly had not studied the sights that I might go to see.

I flew from Adelaide to Melbourne and boarded the 747 for London several hours later. Not liking being crammed into my seat, I spent as much time as possible roaming the aisles and looking out the windows from the various vantage points. There were many other young Australians on the plane who were similarly setting out on the one or two-year expedition; the so-called working holiday.

Some of these young people mentioned that there was a lot of accommodation and many Australians in Earls Court. My knowledge was such that I had never heard of the place but it gave me a destination. This was completely naïve and without prejudice. If someone had told me that there was good cheap accommodation in Finchley I would have gone there.

Once I found my things and made my way through the nightmare that was Heathrow, I boarded a train and was delighted to find that I didn't even have to change as the line went through Earls Court. When I got out of the tube station and walked up the stairs out onto Earls Court Road, I turned left. What urge or instinct drove me I do not know but left was the way I went. Who knows how different things would have been had I turned in the other direction? I walked along the footpath until I came to a sign indicating that there was a backpackers' hostel upstairs. I checked in; initially for one day.

The next morning I paid for another day. This was a ritual I would maintain for a few weeks; until a soldier about to head to Northern Ireland, or his soldier mate, complained about me, or the company I kept, and the place decided it no longer wanted my business.

At first, Earls Court was strangely welcoming. There were many Australians and other colonials around but there were many other groups as well. I found out a little later that the true epicentre of Aussiedom, and probably Kiwidom, was a little further out at Barons Court.

My sheltered existence had, as far as I knew, not brought me into contact with Muslims or the burqa. There were women covered in black and wearing what looked to me like Batman masks and I was told that they were Iranian. I have to admit that I initially found their appearance to be a little unsettling but within a day or so they had become part of the scenery.

That very first afternoon I actually saw a slightly older woman from my home town walking along Earls Court Road. When I say slightly older woman, I mean that she would have been about 23. Her name was Rosemary Woodland and she was strolling past with a group of about five others. I looked at her and she stopped a few metres on, turned around and came back as asked me if I came from Burra. I said that I did. As it happens we had grown up only a few streets from each other. We said hello and wished each other well, and carried on.

The fatefulness of my decision to turn left at the station really began to emerge the second afternoon that I was in London. I purchased a music newspaper or a *Time Out* and started to look for entertainment. I found that Dizzy Gillespie was playing that night at the Albert Hall so I decided that would be my first concert in London.

Time was my own so I didn't head off for the event at the last moment as I would now. I set out some hours before with no real plan on how I would get there. The first pub I came across was the Prince of Teck. Upstairs in the bar there was one young woman and the young barman. I joined them at the bar and consumed a couple of beers before they relaxed enough to go on with the naughty game they had been playing. They had some heroin and had been smoking it; this was known as 'chasing the dragon'. I chatted away vaguely hoping to do a little puffing myself but I just ended up drinking too much and could not make the journey to see the great jazz master. So I adjourned back across the road to my digs having achieved nothing except whetting my appetite for the exotic and forbidden fruit that London had on offer.

Zero Zero and Bramham Gardens

Having arrived in London without even the foggiest of plans, my recreational activities tended to be guided by *Time Out, NME* and *Melody Maker*, the free Australian newspapers, and what people told me in pubs. Which of these was the primary source for my journey to Notting Hill I don't know but I went there on the first Saturday afternoon that I was in London. It was in Notting Hill that I bought my first pot in the English capital.

I walked up the Portobello Road, more or less delighted with the colour and characters. Just the other side of the railway bridge I came across what was meant to be a reggae band. They had just started to play when some guy turned up from a nearby shop with a syndrum. This was a new electronic musical instrument and he had spotted an opportunity to exhibit its possibilities.

Several minutes later, after stuffing around while the modern musical wonder was installed, the band launched back into action. The novelty of the device was too much for the drummer who couldn't resist hitting it: doooh, doooh, do do do, etc. He was clearly really taken with these new sets of sounds but everything else suffered.

This was a lesson for me on the social and aesthetic impacts of new technologies. Eventually, the syndrum found its way into the margins of rock/pop/jazz/reggae music, but the first contact was overwhelming.

While I was still standing there hoping that the syndrumming would settle down so I could enjoy the reggae that the band had to offer, a young West Indian came along and asked me if I wanted to buy £10 of grass. I did, and I was soon puffing away in the street there in my cocoon of ignorance and bravado.

I smoked the African weed over the next few days and when it had run out I asked someone at an Earls Court hotel how I could get some more. He told me about a Spanish guy who had some excellent Moroccan 'zero zero'. I told him I was interested and he set up a night-time meeting on a very black corner a few streets away.

This was asking for trouble but it worked out OK. I'm loitering around the corner of Coleherne Road and Wharfedale Street about 9 pm when a 30 something Spanish guy comes along. After a slightly nervous exchange he shows me some hash. I ask how much. He says £40 an ounce and I agree to buy one.

I had never had so much hash before. Partly this was because of a misunderstanding. If he had said '£10 a quarter', I would have bought that. I later found that quarters of an ounce, or even eights, were the usual quantities for semi-casual users like me. The next day I sealed a little of the hash in plastic and wrapped it in a copy of *Time Out* and posted it back to friends in Australia.

Just at that time I found out that an old mate from Burra was living with his girlfriend in far south-east London. Nigel used to enjoy an occasional puff and I thought I would give him a little treat.

Getting off the tube at Crystal Palace Station I thought 'Desolation Boulevard', but I walked around to the bedsit in a happy frame of mind. There were Nigel and Janine, who appeared to have joined the ski set. In fact, they told me that they had been to Switzerland where their ski gear had been 'stolen' and that had allowed them to stay for an extra month.

I offered them the hash, which was excellent. But they declined. Sort of nervous and embarrassed, I rolled up a small joint myself and lit it up. News travels fast wherever you are and even though I had only been in London a few weeks they had been told about my reportedly wild and dangerous lifestyle. My strange behaviour only confirmed their new image of me.

Pleasantly but substantially intoxicated, I turned on an act for my increasingly uncomfortable audience. Thinking I was being funny, I quickly got to telling them that I was on the improve now and had stopped injecting heroin into my eye. Their looks of shock and disgust told me that the joke had missed its mark. Rather than saying that it was a joke, however, I just finished the little joint, made my excuses and farewells, and headed back to the station. The carriage was almost deserted so I had another sparrow's leg style smoke as I rode back to the northern bank of the Thames.

The source of the reports that had reached Nigel and Janine about my sick and unattractive existence might have been someone at Bramham Gardens, because about the same time that I purchased the hash I met some Aussies who were living there in a large house. There were a variety of connections to various Australians in the building, including the girlfriend of the South African who seemed to own the place. Amanda was also from Burra and I had met her at one of the Tennis Professor's many all-night cricket parties when she was going out with the town's most eligible bikie.

Being flush with money for drinks and having excellent hash for smoking, I quickly had a circle of new friends in Bramham Gardens and began adjourning there regularly after the pub had shut, often bearing a large tin of beer.

It's funny how quickly you settle into places because one night after a session at Bramham Gardens I was walking back tired and drunk when I turned into Earls Court Road nearly in sight of the hostel. 'Home', I thought, as I staggered towards the accommodation. As it happens, this was only a couple of days before I was evicted from my new haven.

Neil and Warren, West Kens'

After my eviction from the hostel I started looking through the free Australian newspapers and on local notice boards trying to find some new digs. Later that morning I found myself not so far away but the other side of the railway line in Avonmore Road, West Kensington. There, two Aussies were looking for someone to help carry the rent load. I won't say that the two were hippies but they displayed some clear hippy traits.

Neil was tall and thin with long hair and he got around in a sarong so the impression of hippyhood was strong. He came from Bunbury in Western Australia and had spent years in India. I think Neil had originally set out to go to India but for some reason or another, he eventually had made his way to London.

Warren sported a more folksy appearance and came from East Gippsland in Victoria. He had also spent quite a while in India but I got the impression that he had travelled to London overland via India, and so on, which had been the style for many Aussies of the previous decade.

Neil and Warren both liked a smoke — hash was the usual fare — and every night was more or less a curry-off. This was the time when I really got used to, and learned to like, strong curries.

Neil was in no hurry to return to Australia, and I'm not sure why, but he did tell me about a misadventure in Western Australia, probably in Perth. One day he and a few of his friends had smoked a lot of grass and drunk a few beers so they thought it would be funny to put on some masks and get around town laughing at the reactions of the people they came across. At one point they went into a shop and got a good laugh and then went into the next building expecting something similar, but it was a bank. The alarm went off and the police arrived and the little group found it very hard to persuade the police that their objectives weren't more sinister.

Neil was a master of living very cheaply and of organising things to best suit himself. If someone announced it was his or her birthday, Neil would say, 'You better buy me a drink then'. When I moved into the flat I got the other bed in Warren's room while Neil had his room to himself until a young Nigerian woman called Barbara Annaba moved in with us. She shared the room with Neil — they got very friendly.

Unloading lorries

The happiest job I ever had was unloading lorries in London. The job started out in an unexceptional manner but it became an absolute joy.

Realising that my frenzy of cash disposal was finite, I decided I needed to enhance my spending power by making some money. Several of the expats that I knew, including Neil and Warren, were getting casual work through an agency called Extraman which was very close to the Kings Head in Earls Court.

The first morning I went there I was told to get into a van parked at the front of the agency. The van took us out to Park Royal where there was a completely nondescript collection of warehouses and lorries.

Ian, a horticulturalist from around Mudgee in New South Wales, drove the van. Then there was Tim Reece, the Englishman from Shepshed in Leicestershire, who was a graduate of Loughborough University of Technology. And the fourth guy was Andy. For someone of my limited experience, the sound and the vision did not compute for Andy because he was a West Indian but spoke with a very strong Glaswegian accent.

When we got to the warehouses we were immediately put to work. We were divided into two groups of two. Ian and Tim were one team and Andy and I were the other. Each pair was taken to a twenty foot shipping container full of boxes of condiments and shown how to pack the boxes onto pallets for the forklift driver to take away.

Andy and I immediately set to work and once we got into a rhythm of unloading we also eased into a steady conversation. Andy lived in Brixton; it sounds stereotypical but it is true. Stereotypes can be true. So I asked him how he came to be working out of an agency in Earls Court and he said that it was much easier to get jobs from there than it was from Brixton. Andy's claim seemed perfectly plausible to me although it was never said if the difference between the two areas' employment opportunities was a matter of race or wealth or something else.

The boxes were really snugly slotted in the shipping container and it took all morning to unpack them but we worked away happily, discussing music and pot, with a little bit of family background thrown in. I couldn't believe how cheap he was getting that African weed, but then again I wasn't really that surprised that there was a different range of commodities and a different price scale down in Brixton. We were not getting exactly the same things, no doubt because of the different lines of supply, but, generally speaking, smoking things cost about half as much in Brixton as they did around SW5 and SW10.

Lunchtime was spent in a transportable hut but it was cosy and warm, there was some edible food and we four casual labourers sat around chatting and having cups of tea. Then the same pairs were directed to new containers and immediately regained our rhythm of work and conversation.

The next day I went to the agency in the morning and was directed straight back to Ian's van to head out to the same job. Once again there were four of us but Andy was not there. In his place was a bearded South African called 'Jo', which might have been short for Johannes.

I didn't have a problem with Jo but I asked Ian what had happened to Andy. Ian said that Andy had not been wanted by the people in the agency, who, I might add, were all either ex-pats or white English. I didn't say anything but I was disgusted. The way we had worked through those containers had meant that the two of us had done exactly the same amount of work and yet they didn't want him — there could be only one reason and it was not a good one.

Strangely enough, I had a very similar experience in Sydney some years later. One morning I got a casual half shift unloading Chinese antique furniture and porcelain, and working with me was an aboriginal lad named Clive. When the half shift was up, one of the owners — they were two English brothers; the Shaws — called me aside and asked me what I thought about working with Clive. I said it was fine. Then he asked me if I wanted to come back after lunch and work the rest of the shift. I said 'Sure', and then he sent me off for my meal break. When I came back Clive had been let go at lunchtime. Once again, this was pure racism because both of us had done exactly the same amount of work.

The second morning that I was at the Royal Park warehouses, the day of Jo's first shift, we were once again immediately set to work unloading shipping containers. This time I was paired with Tim so I didn't get to talk with Jo until that lunch break. Meanwhile, Tim and I chatted away as we worked unloading containers; we got on like a house on fire.

Several times I visited Tim and his girlfriend, Claire, in their basement apartment on the riverside walk between Hammersmith Bridge and the Rutland Hotel. At Loughborough University of Technology, Tim had studied arts. He knew about the notion of 'spectacle' and he told me a lot about obscure bands that he thought I would like. I remember him telling me about Throbbing Gristle and insisting that I should go to see them because I would like the band. I should have taken his advice and seen them in action because I later found Throbbing Gristle to be a very interesting outfit. Some of his other suggestions I did act on and one of these was the Gang of Four, who I saw at the Electric Ballroom in Camden Town.

Once he started working with Ian, Tim, and I, Jo also settled right in. We quickly got into the routine of loading the trucks and rushing back to the warm little room and chatting away; intellectual sort of chats. We all had at least a year or so of university and were interested in culture and politics. We were all very happy and it was a delight to go to work there. At other times or in other places, I would have sat in that room dreading the thought of another lorry coming in to be unloaded but we chatted so furiously that we didn't notice the time and when a lorry did arrive we would race off to do the unloading as quickly as possible so we could continue our conversation.

A lot of the stuff that we unloaded seemed to come from the subcontinent. Whole twenty or even forty-foot containers filled with sacks of spices came in quite regularly. There was one little trick to the sacks that Jo couldn't get. If the sacks were stacked on the pallet one directly on top of the other then the pallet would be unstable and the sacks would fall off. However, if you loaded the successive layers of sacks in opposite directions then the whole lot would be interwoven and stable.

When the first container of sacks arrived all four of us started unloading it but a problem became apparent immediately. Jo would get a sack, carry it to the pallet, stand there and think, and then put the sack the same way as the one underneath (exactly as it was not supposed to go), so he would have to move it again. Then he would go through the whole routine again, thinking even longer this time, but producing the same result. We soon told him to stand aside because he was just slowing us other three. Subsequently, whenever there was a container of sacks to be unloaded we would just send Jo back to the hut.

Jo was dyslexic and his life expectancy in the job appeared very limited. We were there to unload the lorries as they arrived and they often contained sacks and Jo was a liability in the sack-unloading department. He might not have lasted beyond his first day but while he was standing there keeping out of the way a lorry came in with a French driver. Overhearing the attempts of the driver and the foreman to communicate, Jo went over and translated. Jo was fluent in seven European languages and he proved very handy. The next day a Spanish driver arrived and Jo was immediately sent for, as he was for all foreign language drivers after that while he worked with us at the Park Royal warehouses.

Day after day the four of us rode out in the little van. It was obvious how well we all got on and how happy we were. Our cheer was such that it seemed to have lifted the mood of the whole works. One afternoon, however, the foreman called us in and told us that we would not be needed the next day, nor for the indefinite future. We were very disappointed and the foreman was almost crying.

Carnivals, Nazis, police and Elvis Costello

While the casual observer would have been hard pressed to see it, one of the main motivations for my trip to London was an interest in politics. Outside of the conversations in the workmen's hut at the Park Royal warehouses, one of the few obvious signs of that interest was my participation in rallies and riots in south London and Notting Hill.

I went to two carnivals at Notting Hill, more or less hoping that they would turn into riots as they had done in previous years, and was not disappointed. At my first Notting Hill Carnival in 1979, I wandered around soaking up the atmosphere, watching the guys mixing and scratching reggae as people moved to the rhythms. The sounds and the colours were great. I felt right at home and unthreatened. I liked the carnival and I liked the area so much that I often thought about moving up to Notting Hill or Ladbroke Grove but for one reason or another it didn't happen.

The first carnival was the most exciting, and for someone like me who was looking for a riot, it was interesting to see how quickly, and seemingly spontaneously, it developed. I could feel the excitement building. There was a tension and an anticipation that was happy but getting more and more fraught.

Well into the afternoon, some minor disturbance got a few guys running. As soon as the energy was made manifest in that way, it spread through the crowd. Adrenalin was about and I found myself running around just as hundreds of others were doing.

Clearly the fire was already in the air, or in the backs of people's minds, otherwise the whole thing wouldn't have taken off as quickly as it did. The running around was fun. I didn't see any great violence or damage and soon enough the police were able to divide us into smaller, less energetic and dangerous groups, until I was isolated with a few others. Then it was simply a case of slowing to a walk and casually sauntering down to Notting Hill Gate Station to get the tube home.

The first year I was at the carnival, the outbreak of the 'riot' seemed spontaneous but there must have been a lot of people, like myself, who anticipated or even hoped that there might be such action. I'm not sure if there were any agitators as such. I didn't see any, but it is possible that there were people trying to get things going.

There was, of course, little that was spontaneous about the police presence or the way that the authorities broke down the riot. They were prepared and in a few hours they were well and truly back in the drivers' seat.

The following year, the process and my participation in it was much the same, but the whole thing was compressed. There could be a variety of reasons for that. One might simply have been that the underlying tension, that fused joy and anger, was simply less intense. Another is much more certain.

While the carnival was in full swing in 1980, I went for a walk around Ladbroke Grove. As soon as I got a couple streets away from Portobello Road, I came across lines of vans and hundreds of police. There were whole streets of police vehicles in position, waiting for the action to begin. No doubt they had studied the happenings of the previous years and I think they had learnt quite well, because the process of neutralising the excited but directionless mob by dividing it into smaller and smaller groups seemed to succeed much more quickly that it had the year before. I felt that I did much less running around in 1980 before it was time to walk down to the station and catch the tube back to Earls Court.

The 'rioting' at Notting Hill was interesting, I enjoyed the excitement and the resistance implied in it, but there was more serious action on the other side of London. This was the time of the National Front and of the Anti-Nazi League. I didn't know it at the time, but this was the twilight of the Anti-Nazi League era. The National Front and the Anti-Nazi League would schedule simultaneous rallies. The rallies were simultaneous, but the scheduling was not because the fascists would plan to exercise their democratic rights and then the anti-fascists would set their event for the same time and place. This later move was undoubtedly provocative, but so was the initial one because the National Front consistently held their meetings in working class areas with large, non-white, immigrant populations.

The first time I went to one of these south London events I managed to see a little action. The group that I found myself in got quite near to the fascists before the police cut us off and forced us away from the continuing confrontation.

On that occasion I was really struck by the huge blocks of Council housing. I was surprised, even a little shocked by the environment. Seeing these heavily populated domestic suburbs disturbed me. I began to wonder whether I should be there at all because I was just playing a kind of political game while the people who lived there were coping with, and were going to have to continue to cope with, this reality. In the second Anti-Nazi League rally that I attended there was a sight that really cemented that feeling, which was really one of disillusionment and loss of direction.

I'm not sure exactly where the second of these rallies took place. It could have been Lambeth but it was certainly near Elephant and Castle. Once again this was a situation where the National Front had planned a rally in a poor London suburb with a substantial ethnic population and then the Anti-Nazi League had responded by scheduling their gathering in the same location at the same time.

One of the ironies of these organised confrontations was that you would find yourself travelling to the site with your planned opponents. I remember being in a tube carriage where there were about ten skinheads covered in Union Jacks and racist paraphernalia. I was grateful that they were not mind-readers and didn't know I was going down to join their opponents. As I looked about the carriage I saw a few other young guys that might also have been joining us. One pair that looked to me like potential Anti-Nazi League supporters was completely surrounded by skinheads; they were sitting quietly and keeping pretty much to themselves.

When we got down to Lambeth, if it was Lambeth, the police identified the non-Nazis and kept us away. We found ourselves wandering around back and side streets but from whichever way we approached the National Front rally and our planned confrontation, the group that fate put me in was constantly thwarted. I assume that the police were there to keep the peace by stopping us anti-Nazis from attacking those skinheads and their legitimate political activity, but their defence seemed a little too enthusiastic. I distinctly remember a few of us turning into one of those grey back streets only to be confronted by a rank of about twenty police with a couple on horseback. As we approached, one thuggy cop at the front said to me and the few others, 'I hope you've got your boots on boys. We have'.

My second Anti-Nazi League rally was a complete non-event insofar as my efforts to reach the action proved futile, but in other ways the learning experience was very interesting.

Continually being turned away from the planned events, I found myself going through or around Elephant and Castle on a few different occasions from a couple of different directions. On one of these sorties I noticed Elvis Costello walking past. 'Noticed' is an understatement. Elvis Costello was dressed from head to toe in canary yellow. To give the picture in a little more detail: he was wearing a yellow suit with a yellow shirt and a yellow tie, while strolling along in his patent leather yellow shoes and yellow socks. His belt was also yellow as was anything else he was wearing that was visible. I assume he was going where I wanted to go but had a pass. I had to admit, though, that he was making a political statement by declaring his presence loudly and clearly.

A little later, as I was rounding another corner in Elephant and Castle I came across a group of weird Nazis. Perhaps I shouldn't be judgmental about this sort of thing, but this group of between a dozen and a score of mainly young men were all in black leather and shiny silver metal. They were rounding the corner on the other side of the street, and they were covered in Nazi regalia. I didn't know whether to be scared or revolted or to burst out laughing. Almost instantly, before I had time to formulate my response, a group of West Indian youths and young men stopped the ridiculous troop of highly decorated souvenir collectors. The young West Indians had no doubt about their response and immediately sprinted towards the fascist troop. I've got to admit I was delighted and I laughed as the Nazis tried to run off in their black leather boots, trousers, jackets and caps with all their metal work jingling and gangling about. There were fewer of the West Indians than there were members of the Nazi regalia gang and they stopped chasing them well before their prey stopped running, but the message had been delivered.

The West Indian lads had not been part of the Anti-Nazi League rally that day but their communication was much more effective. At that point I felt like a spectator. I decided that the locals were much better equipped to do what had to be done about the fascists than I was with my romantic and spectatorial games.

The Coke factory

Back in the flat at Avonmore Road, rules were on. Every morning began with a cup of tea and a bong, and then we were straight into the van for the drive out to the Coke factory. I was always the last one up. Neil and Warren would already be sitting at the table, and the latter, who was more organised, would have the cup of tea and the packed bong waiting for me.

With the three of us jammed in the front, Warren drove the van to the Coke factory, which would take a good forty minutes. We worked an odd shift from 11am to 8pm. I'm fairly sure that the management really only wanted us for the last four hours, when we would man the production line, and only had us cleaning up a warehouse for the first half of the shift to have us fill in time in a useful-looking way.

The warehouse we were cleaning was full of old soft drinks, mainly in small bottles. It seemed to be a kind of graveyard for semi-retired beverages. We swept and hosed the place day after day for no apparent reason and there was no one on our backs to make us overly productive. Most of the time we just amused ourselves talking and smoking.

In our exploration of the warehouse, we found that there was a batch of drinks that had fermented. We discovered this first from the mess and later from the way that the bottles would easily crack. Once we had found the fermented or re-fermented drinks we had to give them a go. They were more or less unpalatable but one day we did drink enough to be slightly drunk on the premises.

During the first half of our odd shift, when we weren't cleaning up the storage building, we walked about doing odd jobs. The facility had some interesting cultural idiosyncrasies. The whole place's full-time staff was divided on racial lines. The overseers and the tradesmen were white Englishmen. The production line was the only racially mixed area and all of the forklift drivers were West Indian. To this you could have added that all the casual employees were colonials. Everyone was male apart from a couple of the production line watchers.

You only needed to know one word to get around the place; 'alright'. Whenever two employees met one would say 'Alright', and the other would then respond, 'Alright'. Of course, the exchange is slightly misrepresented because one was a question and the other an answer: 'Alright?' 'Alright'.

In the second half of the shift, Warren, Neil and I either watched the production line or, more likely, loaded component materials onto it. The production line was almost fail-safe but it was the job of several people to watch at the points where something could go wrong and ensure that it didn't. Strangely enough, every single evening some things would go wrong and bring the whole process to a halt. Everyone liked the break so if it wasn't the unsaid responsibility of everyone to ensure that breakdowns happened every day, there were enough willing takers to guarantee that it did. The resultant breakdowns were never planned and never mentioned and yet they happened on every shift.

It is hard to explain this silent conspiracy and understanding without referring to a couple of specific examples. Two of these relate at least partially to the same point in the process.

26

1. *The invisible bottle top.*

It was the job of one employee to monitor the soft drink bottles as they moved along the production line at the point preceding their filling. Every now and then a bottle would come along with a top on it. The employee would be there precisely to ensure such bottles were removed before they reached the filling machine. For a bottle with a top on to reach the filling machine the attendant would have had to ignore it for about 30 seconds, and yet, whenever there was an occasional topped bottle one would somehow get through and bring the whole process to a standstill.

The employee had to have stood there being wilfully blind and unresponsive. I can only guess that the managers were so above the operations of the slaves on the factory floor that they didn't know what was required for the plant to break down as often as it did.

2. *Lazy bottles.*

At the same point in the production line the odd bottle would come along lying down rather than standing. The monitoring employee was supposed to stand these bottles up before they reached the filling machine and yet, somehow, about once a shift one prostate bottle would get through and we would have another smoko while the tradesman got the plant going again.

There was a very similar situation the other side of the filling machine. Every now and then a bottle would fall over in the filling process and it would be the job of the next monitoring employee to remove the bottle before it reached the capping machine. These 'lazy' bottles would only appear very infrequently, and still, if any did appear one would get through and upset the applecart, and we would all have to stand around doing nothing once again.

3. The wall of glass.

The most spectacular and obvious version of this shared, unsaid and wilful failure that I saw took place where the crates of bottles were loaded. Just outside the factory there was a tray of rollers onto which whole pallets of clean bottles would be placed by a forklift. The mechanical rollers would then move the stack inside the building where another machine would remove the bottles and put them onto the production line. Sometimes all the bottles were new and sometimes they were all recycled ones that had been cleaned. That is how the odd one with a top on sometimes appeared.

One evening, all the bottles were new. I think that the pallets of bottles would be about eight crates high. The crucial thing was that alternate layers of crates would be arranged in opposite directions. This meant that the crates were interlocked in the way that bricks usually are. This particular evening, however, pallets of new bottles were arriving in which each layer was exactly the same as all the others. In effect, the whole pallets were composed of towers of crates, with each tower consisting of eight crates one on top of the other.

These pallets were loaded onto the conveyer. Then, as soon as the rollers jerked into action the last row of crates would fall off the back of the pallet. A wall of crates filled with new bottles would fall onto the wet concrete while we stood and watched. Most of the bottles would smash leaving a terrible mess of shiny wet glass that we would clean up. Then we would put the remaining bottles and crates back on the machine. It would jerk into action, a wall of glass bottles would fall off the back and so on. Eventually, that pallet, or a small portion of it, would make it inside the factory and the next pallet of new bottles would be loaded onto the rollers for the whole process to start again.

The forklift driver and the labourers there to facilitate the operation could all see what was happening and why. We could have rearranged some of the crates to make the pallets more stable, but no one did. We stood and watched and cleaned up without comment; going about our jobs, mindlessly as it were, and extremely inefficiently.

Montséret

Sweeping and talking in the Coke factory's small bottles retirement home one dull and drizzly afternoon, Neil observed that he would rather be outside in the sun. Warren pointed out that we were at the beginning of the grape season in southern France and pickers got 17 francs per hour. This was more than we were making hanging around at the Coke factory and the more we talked about it the more attractive the option became. Over the next day or so we talked ourselves into the idea and then we booked a trip on Magic Bus to Perpignan, which is right down at the bottom of France near the Mediterranean coast, in sight of the Pyrenees, and, therefore, Spain.

Magic Bus was then a no frills operation that seemed to string together passenger loads using the cheapest local contractors. The journey proceeded well enough until we got to a junction about fifteen kilometres south of Narbonne when the driver stopped the bus and announced that he was going in a different direction. The remaining passengers, of which there were about a dozen, would have to get out here, he said.

We all argued but seemed to have little choice and soon found ourselves with our possessions to the south of Narbonne on the side of the A9 near the junction with the A61. Our immediate mission was now to hitch the sixty-odd kilometres down to Perpignan. A couple of the other groups got rides before a thirty-something rural Frenchman in a van picked up Neil, Warren and I. We managed to convey our destination but the rest of the conversation was very limited and soon enough we all stopped trying.

In Perpignan we booked into a hostel that held a dozen or more other potential grape pickers. We were told that the season was quite well advanced but growers were still coming in at a reasonable rate. You simply had to wait your turn and you would get work.

Walking about Perpignan in the sun was a welcome change from London's dreary weather and the Coke factory's grey innards. One of the first things that I noticed was that steak and chips was probably the most common meal taken by the outside diners. And, unlike the so-called French fries of some restaurant franchises, these were big, crisp, chunky, chips.

That night back at the hostel someone told us about a kind of speakeasy where you could buy very cheap homemade beer. So we headed off to this nondescript door in a little side street and knocked. The young French guy who answered the door was mainly concerned to know if we had bottles to exchange as it was even cheaper if you had replacement bottles to fill. We didn't but we bought three large bottles of beer. They were only a couple of francs each and the beer was a very good larger. You don't hear much about French beers but the ones I had in Perpignan and then later in Montséret and Paris were all good.

On the second day that we were in the Perpignan hostel, a woman in her late sixties turned up looking for three pickers. Warren, Neil and I were more or less next in line so we were picked. We had very little French and she didn't have much English, but as we were putting our things into her little Citroen she did say 'No holiday'.

The vineyard was much further from Perpignan than we expected and I got the impression that we might have been nearer to Narbonne. Later I found that we could have walked the dozen

31

kilometres west northwest to the junction where the Magic Bus had prematurely discharged us beside the road.

We were going to be picking grapes for the Moreau family. The family only had three members. There was the grandmother who had picked us up, the father, who was in his early forties and seemed nice enough, and a very attractive girl in her late teens, a classic French farmer's daughter. We had very little to do with any of them except the grand Madame who ran the show.

The Moreau's winery and vineyards were near Montséret, which is a little village of only a few hundred people. The village lies beneath a very interestingly shaped hill, with a steep face of broken stone boulders rising to a peak over the town and then gradually sloping away to the north east. I assume this distinctive weathered geological eruption is the Mont that gave the village its name.

We were shown to our digs, which was a simple old two-room house about 150 metres from Moreau's main farmhouse and winery. The cottage was very basic but reasonably comfortable and more or less fit our preconceptions, insofar as we had any. Anyone touched with a romantic yearning for historic provincial France might have been delighted by it.

As soon as we had settled in we headed off to town to buy some necessities. There were only two tiny little shops in town. There were two middle-aged women in the one we went into. The shopkeeper inside was talking to another woman who seemed to be combining a little shopping with casual socialising. As soon as we entered the shop the two women were very keen to talk to us.

They had as much English as we had French but they enthusiastically tried to be helpful and to engage us in conversation. The two women wanted to know where we were from and if we were there to pick grapes. All of that was good and very friendly. Then they asked us which family we were picking for and we said the Moreaus. As soon as we did the whole tone changed. 'Oh, Moreaus', was followed by an awkward silence from both the women.

Once that hurdle was over we went back to the conversation and trying to buy the groceries. We communicated our needs as much by gesture and mimicking sounds as we did with actual words but managed to get everything we wanted except the honey. This proved quite a challenge. At one point Warren's buzzing sound led the shopkeeper to go out through the back door into her residence and reappear with a can of insect spray. We were all laughing and after a few more attempts she retreated again into her domicile and came out with the small half-jar of honey from her own table. She was insisting we have it but we couldn't take it.

Most of the wine growers in Montséret sold their grapes to the town's cooperative but the Moreaus made their own. They seemed to be the richest family in town. The Moreaus owned a consolidated vineyard of several lots but they also had other isolated individual fields of grapes scattered all round the village. I guessed that over the years this wealthier family had bought one block of vines after another as circumstances led to their sale.

The morning after we arrived in Montséret we met with the other workers in front of the winery where we all climbed onto little grape carts pulled by a tractor. After a few minutes ride we arrived at the vines to be picked and were immediately set to work. Almost all the other workers were Portuguese who were working through their summer holidays.

Many of the lots that we picked contained very old vines. Rather than being on trellises, these were all gnarled bushes low to the ground. It was backbreaking work.

Almost all the grapes were a red variety, I would guess something like Syrah, but every now and then one of the bushes would be of a white variety. We pickers often refreshed ourselves from the hot sun by sampling the juice from some of these white grapes. At times you would be hot and looking out for the next white vine.

The work was very hard but the scenery was great and initially we enjoyed our changed circumstances. We had imagined ourselves doing this and here we were. The work itself was pleasant enough to begin with, even despite the bending and the heat, but some problems soon emerged.

Not for the first time, and nor for the last, I was too thorough and therefore too slow in my work. I was working hard but with each of the pickers going along their own row of vines I constantly found myself to be the last in the line of the dozen pickers. I should have sped up by ignoring the more underground of the grapes but didn't and I caught Madame Moreau's eye at the back of the pack.

The grand dame was not one to tolerate such things for very long and after a day or two she moved me from picking to carrying the picked grapes and dumping them in the carts. Carrying was actually a higher paid job and that meant one of the regular Portuguese workers would now get two or three francs less per hour. You can imagine how that went down. He was not happy but Madame Moreau was not inclined to bend, and he knew it.

The next hiccup was the wine. As part of their work conditions, grape pickers in France were entitled to a wine ration. Pickers were allowed about 1.5 litres per day and carriers a little more. We were given wine all right but it was dark, thick and bitter with a lot of sediment. To me it was like the skins were brewed up after the juice from the first pressing had been taken for the good stuff.

We complained about the poor quality wine but Monsieur Moreau told us that this was the very same as that the family themselves drank. We did not believe that for one second but there seemed to be little that we could do about it. After we had finished work on the second or third afternoon we walked the little more than two kilometres to the next village of Saint-André-de-Roquelongue. There we found that the local Co-op produced an exceptional rosé that was inexpensive. From then on we took the walk almost daily, wandering along the Rue de Musée beside the spectacular outcrop and its ruined chateau to get a couple of chilled bottles of the excellent rosé. The Moreaus had done us a favour, although that was hardly the intent.

It wasn't long before another problem began to emerge. We were hauled to and from the vineyards by a tractor pulling the little carts that carried the grapes back to the winery. This meant that we all had to assemble in time to be picked up in the morning and we didn't return until Madame Moreau said so. We were supposed to finish at 5pm but right from the start we worked a minute or two longer and within a few days the extra time had begun to stretch out.

There were exchanged looks and glances at watches but Madame Moreau was impervious to such frivolities. It quickly became clear that the Portuguese, while unhappy, were not going to say anything. We tolerated it through the first week but it only got worse in the next one. Finally, on the Friday of our second week, when the clock had clearly ticked over past five thirty, Warren said it was time to stop. Madame Moreau argued but so did we. The others said nothing but that was the end of the day's work.

We complained again when we got back to the winery but were told to like it or lump it; or French words to that effect. The three of us resigned.

We had been warned that the employers might try to keep a percentage of the pay, claiming they had to retain it for tax purposes. We had been told that they were not required or even entitled to keep the percentage but that it was a common practice by unscrupulous employers accustomed to getting every franc out of their ignorant and/or intimidated workers. So it came as no surprise when the Moreaus did it to us. We argued and complained but could not get anywhere. We didn't know where to turn to get our full entitlement and in the end we wasted our breath because the ten percent was deducted. It is very frustrating when you know that you are being diddled but you still can't do anything about it.

This was Friday evening and both parties wanted us gone ASAP but, due to the limited transport options, we had to stay until Sunday morning. Consequently, we were in Montséret on the Saturday with nothing to do but to fill our day with leisure. We decided to climb up the mount that overlooked the town to examine the remains of the chateau and to take in the view. When we got to the peak we smoked chillums of hash and enjoyed the wonderful scenery. The Pyrenees were clearly visible and so were teams of workers picking grapes in the vineyards around the village. We could see that the group immediately below the Mont was Madame Moreau's charges. Soaking in the blue hues of the distant mountains and not labouring under the grand dame, was a wonderful moment in which the feeling of freedom was intense.

The next day we were dropped at the nearest railway station. From there we caught the local train to Narbonne. Then we boarded the train from Narbonne to Lyon, which was a more modern affair and took us through the important and picturesque tourist city of Carcassonne. The inside of the train is as close as I have ever been to the wonderful fortified Cité de Carcassonne, but at least we could see it.

In Lyon we went to a café for lunch. We were sitting there eating pastries and drinking coffee when three young Australians came in. They were rude, loud and obnoxious. They were vocally rubbishing the other people in the café, especially the staff, and French people generally. We just kept quiet.

Then we went back to the station and caught the next train to Paris. The step up from the local train to the intercity one was marked but this next train was a new experience for us all. The train from Lyon to Paris was a very modern, fast, tilt train, and we had not been on anything quite like it. Smoothly and quietly it jetted thorough the French countryside.

Neil, Warren and I were familiar with the country trains in Australia where you could hang around smoking near the rattling doors at the end of the carriages. We decided to have a hash joint and adjourned to the end section of the carriage. The compartments in these carriages, however, were hermetically sealed by electric doors, and the sections near the carriage doors were divided from the seating area by glass walls. Rather than being hidden from view with the fumes being drawn out of the carriage, we were in plain sight of the other passengers. As we smoked the hash, the little airlock-like compartment filled with smoke. Then, when the door was activated so we could re-enter, a cloud of hash smoke billowed into the carriage. We couldn't help but laugh as we stumbled back in through the smoke.

Once in Paris we set about finding accommodation for the night. Given that we were going to catch a train to London from la Gare du Nord the next morning, we found a cheap room near there. The room was cheap enough but it needed to be. There were holes in the toilet doors and trails of blood on the ceiling of our room that had obviously come out of a syringe.

The biggest lump of coke

Back in London a little flusher, Warren, Neil and I decided to hold a party at our cosy flat in Avonmore Road. This was an ambitious exercise because if people were packed like cattle into the living area (that is, the kitchen) there would be room for a total of about a dozen. Given that was the result, we regarded the party as a success.

The function involved a few furious hours of alcohol, cigarettes and pot, and a wall of loud, animated, competing, conversations of which I can recall very little. But the occasion was very memorable for a couple of reasons.

As a very special treat to enhance the festivities, we three hosts had purchased a little coke. We were at the very bottom of the food chain for anything more exotic than smoke so we were lucky not to get complete rubbish. What we ended up with was a powder that had some coke in it but also a little speed to give it a kick that would simulate a much more concentrated blend of cocaine.

One of our guests was a kiwi named Pat. Pat had been a wool classer in NZ but in the UK he had become a purveyor of recreational-substances, mainly, but not exclusively, hash. Not long after Pat turned up we offered him a little snort. I warned him that it was cut but when I explained that it had a little speed in it he went ahead and had his line or two. The dialogue that followed was one of the reasons why I'm confident that there was at least a reasonable amount of coke in the mix and also one of the reasons why I've since shied away from the stuff and its users.

Once the gear had kicked in, Pat started on a line of conversation with the primary and recurring theme being why he, Pat, was so good and successful, and why I wasn't; in fact, why I was pretty much a loser. Strangely enough, this derogatory near-monologue was conducted in good humour. You could say that he was full of himself, or you could say he was full of coke, or full of it.

Later on, as Pat was leaving I made some witty remark. I wish I could remember what I said but I have never been able to. What I do recall was that Pat fell over backwards laughing, literally. When he had regathered himself, he got up and pulled out what was the biggest lump of coke that I had ever seen. Pat then broke off a chunk and gave me the biggest lump of coke that I've ever possessed, before he remade his farewells and headed out the door.

Neil and I were surprised and excited. We rushed in and roused Warren, who had already gone to bed. The party was winding down but the few who remained, especially Warren, Neil and I, made short work of the coke.

About a year or so after this West Kens' party, a few of us went to visit Pat after he had moved into a room in a five storey terrace in Drayton Gardens, which is a little past The Boltons, on the Chelsea side. Just as we reached the front of the building, a cab turned up and Pat jumped out, saying, 'Hold this will you?' As I stuffed the package under my jacket I noticed that it contained a block of about a kilo or so of Moroccan red.

This was only a momentary thing and I gave the block back before we entered the building. Another time, however, I was in the Kings Head and Donald Purvis came in and said he was afraid that he was going to be searched. So I accepted the package, slipped out the other door and made my circuitous way back to his place. I dare not think about what was in that package or how my explanation would have washed.

My job at Honda

After a series of jobs with Extraman, including the one at the Coke factory with my flatmates, one morning I found myself being driven out to Chiswick where there were two Honda warehouses. The warehouses were highly casualised. There were a few permanent positions, including the managers, but most of their shop floor workforce was provided by Extraman, and it consisted almost entirely of the usual assortment of colonial expats.

The driver of the van that took us to and from the warehouses was Bob, a little Aussie from Melbourne. Bob had a sort of screwed up expression and thick glasses. He was a nice, quiet guy. He still enjoyed a drink with the boys, and sometimes haunted the colonial hotels, where he sensibly would only have a few. He had been in London for seven years so one day, when I saw we were sharing a urinal in one of the Aussie pubs, I asked Bob if he was going to stay in London. He was outraged. Bob declared that he was an Australian and to Australia he would return. I wonder whether he ever did.

The Honda warehouses might be thought of as gigantic filing cabinets where what were filed were not documents but car or motorcycle parts. What most of the casual workers did at these warehouses was to put new parts out into their appropriate places or to collect new parts from those places and combine them with others making up orders for Honda sellers and repairers all over the UK.

We were like ants moving parts around inside this large pair of connected nests. Our soundtrack was Capitol Radio, which seemed to be designed to drive the toiling inhabitants into a semi-hypnotised daze. Every hour, or so it seemed, the same 'Top Ten' songs would be played. And every hour there would also be a golden oldie, which was usually from last week's Top Ten, or a 'Prediction' that would be from next week's relentless rotation. While I was there, Blondie's 'Atomic' and The Pretenders' 'Brass in Pocket' were on the short playlist; and they still transport me back to the Honda innards.

Fate, or what seems like fate, is a funny thing and it appears that my portion there was meant to be strange. Who knows, I might be imagining it but my job at Chiswick was unusual in a number of ways and right from the start I was given the odd tasks. The very first day that I was at the Honda warehouses, I was given a job that was kind of the underbelly, flipside, or accident of the others' work. I was shown a pile of returned parts. These returns were mainly the products of mistaken orders and I was given the job of putting the parts back into their proper places.

After a couple of days I had re-filed all the returned parts so then I was given the task of disposing of damaged or excess stock. This job really surprised me. I was a bit shocked and a little disgusted with how the whole thing worked.

I was taken to a vacant old brick-paved area near the Power Road entrance of the car warehouse where there was a skip. I was given a knife, a crowbar and a sledgehammer, directed to a pile of parts, and told these things had to go. I was to render them completely unsalable, and once each part was put into this desired state I was to throw it into the skip.

It was understandable that you would get rid of damaged stock but I think that the public would have been surprised at the level of expediency. Owners of new Preludes and Accords might well have been scandalized to find that a brand new car panel that had a superficial scratch, not even a scratch through to the metal, but a scratch through the outer layer of undercoat to the layer beneath, rendered the part surplus so it had to be trashed.

Time was equally savage. The warehouse only kept parts until models were five years out of date. Then all the parts for those models were destroyed and thrown out. Any excess orders that arrived from the main European distribution centre in Frankfurt similarly had to go.

Initially, I found the job of contrived destruction more enjoyable than the part filing, and it was better to be outside, but it didn't feel right to be scratching and denting new car panels or to be cutting holes in perfectly good car seats. Nevertheless, I faithfully soldiered on, often putting on a particularly violent display when one of the managers appeared. Even so, I remained uneasy and I tried a number of tactics, I suppose, to make me feel better about things.

First, I set out to expose the operation. There was a driveway of about ten metres between two buildings that led to my little area of destruction beside the skip. The driveway came from Power Road and on the other side of the road there was a BBC facility. The BBC staff used to pile out of their workplace one hour and fifteen minutes before we would clock off. So, I would save a particularly juicy piece, perhaps a panel from the current model Accord that had the most superficial of damage. I would place the piece at the extremity of my work area nearest to the road where the BBC workers would pass and then, when they were going past, I would destroy the piece in as loud and as dramatic a manner as I could muster.

No one noticed. Or, if they did, they just noticed a horrible noisy worker and they did their best to ignore him. The whole exercise was futile but I persisted with it. At first, I did so because it made me feel a bit better but I should have stopped because it began to entrench a kind of bitterness.

I also tried to think of ways to save and use some of these things that were being destroyed and discarded, but car parts are pretty much specific to their place and purpose so there was not much that I could do. One day, however, I did find myself carrying a car seat as I was squeezing into the van with about ten other guys for the trip back to Earls Court. Then I walked home with the seat that ended up as a kind of TV chair in our little flat in Avonmore Road.

If this job was soul-destroying it could also be futile and ridiculous. One day a manager came out to find me busily stabbing a large group of car seats with my knife. As usual I was hamming it up, trying to make my assault on the seats look as much as possible like a commuter's New York subway nightmare as it might have been filmed by Fritz Lang in black and white with lots of diagonals and an unsteady camera. Anyway, much to my surprise the manager was surprised and demanded that I stop immediately. 'They're out of the new Prelude', he said, and told me to leave the rest of the seats until he returned. Then he strode off to the main office. About fifteen minutes later he was back, saying that too many had been ordered from Frankfurt, so I was to continue with my assault. Not that he put it exactly like that.

This being a largely pre-personal-and-small-business-computer-era, I hadn't heard the expression 'fat finger mistake', but the thing itself certainly already existed. One day a whole lorry load of shock absorbers was dumped next to the skip. There had been an order of shockies that was ten times too big. The exact figure eludes me but it was something like 1000 shock absorbers had been ordered when 100 was the total storage capacity.

This challenge was too much. Shock absorbers are made to be tough and my simple tools — the knife, bar and hammer — weren't up to the job. The best I could do was to put a few scratches onto the shock absorbers. But even scratched they still would have been perfectly serviceable brand new shockies, just very slightly defaced. I reported my failure to the manager. After a brief quizzical scrutiny of the evidence he accepted the gravity of my situation and told me just to throw them into the skip. This took a couple of days because there was more than one whole skip load of shock absorbers.

After a week or two as a destroy-and-dispose-man, I had worked myself out of a job. The pile of things to go had gone but the stack of things to go back had been replenished, so I was put back on my returns duty. I had been a reasonably good if melodramatic worker up till this point but things were about to go downhill.

The job of returns-man had two peculiarities, benefits if you like, that I would exploit. The first oddity was the freedom of movement. Almost all the casual workers had jobs filing new parts or collecting them for orders. Most were doing this in the car warehouse but a smaller group did it in the motorcycle warehouse, which was the other side of Gunnersbury Avenue. Either way, each of the other casual workers was confined to just one of the distribution buildings.

The returns person, however, usually served that function in both warehouses. This arose from the fact that, for a reason I never knew, some of the returned lots included motorcycle parts in with the car ones. The result was that the returns person, me, could freely move from one site to the other. If I wasn't in one building then it would just be assumed that I was in the other.

The freedom of movement was the first ingredient that would form part of my constellation of irresponsible non-work exploitation. I could wander around at will and very quickly I fell into the habit of going for mid-morning and mid-afternoon walks a few hundred metres along Chiswick High Road to the shops near the station. It's not that I did anything wrong there. Rather, I've always liked walking and the crime or sin if you like in these two strolls was simply that I was absent from my work and therefore not doing what I was being paid to do.

The next component of my coming passive sabotage was a matter of timeliness. Dealerships and repairers were waiting for the new parts and so the orders had to be completed in a reasonably short time. Similarly, the loads of new parts that arrived at the warehouses (all of which seemed to come from the main European distribution centre in Frankfurt) would be infrequent but large and management would be aware of how long it would take for them to be filed away. The returned parts, however, arrived as unique batches in an irregular and ad hoc manner. None of the supervisory staff kept track of how many returned parts arrived and how many were for the car warehouse, or how many needed to be taken over the road to the motorcycle warehouse. The manager would notice the pile of returns, but he would not really take stock of how much had been added to or taken from the mound. So long as the pile existed there was a need for a returns man.

If one were inclined to laziness, as I was very much at the time, then the job facilitated it. A returns-person was not needed all the time because, even though there was a very bumpy flow of returns, the average flow was considerably less than could be managed in a single full-time position. So, the lazy person could put some things away and wander down the street and otherwise take it easy, and still the stack of returns would remain within the bounds of the unexceptional. This meant that my new habit of strolling morning and afternoon could easily be accommodated in the job.

It was nearly Christmas, it might even have been the last day before the Christmas holidays, and I was in the middle of my mid-afternoon stroll, casually making my way back to the car parts warehouse, when a few flakes of snow appeared. It was a lovely moment and I wandered back with a heart that was full, or fuller.

The next break-through in my plunge toward extreme indolence was a discovery I made up in the bench seat section of the car parts warehouse. The bench seats came in individual cardboard cartons and these were stacked about ten high. Some cunning soul had arranged the stacks of one of the kinds of bench seats so that there was a bench seat surrounded on all sides by these boxes. If you came in from the row behind and climbed diagonally over the back of that section you found yourself in a snug, discrete, little cavity. A bench seat was at the bottom of this nook. Scattered around the seat at the base of the hide were a few empty drink

45

containers and a couple of food wrappers, but their arrangement and the dust told me that this casual rest facility had not been used for some time.

I took to having a little lie down, even a sleep, up in the hollow on the Prelude bench seat. In fact, my morning routine quickly became this: I would turn up with the others in the van and clock in; then I would do a quick lap of the car distribution building, making my circuitous way to the bench seat rest bay, where I would doze off for a while; and finally, refreshed, I would then walk over to the motorcycle parts warehouse and return in time for lunch. I enjoyed the walking, but I was also making sure that I had been seen around the place so no one's suspicions would be raised.

I was already a duplicitous industrial liability but things were going to get worse. The casual workers at Honda had to clock in and clock out. We would all clock in as soon as we got out of the van in the morning and then at the end of the day we would mill around for about ten minutes waiting for time so we could punch our cards into the machine and jump into the van. Employees were also supposed to clock out and back in again at lunchtime. The employees who didn't go out for lunch, however, just double-clicked their cards at the beginning of the break.

This was the last piece of the jigsaw. I already had my morning circuit and snooze, and my afternoon constitutional, and now I added a continental lunch break. When lunchtime came I would double-click my card, as if I was staying in for lunch, but then walk down to Gunnersbury Station. I would catch the train back to West Kens' (it went straight there) and go home for lunch. After I had cooked myself a substantial lunch, I sat around watching television and having cups of tea and maybe even a bong. Fully rested and recharged, I would head off and catch the tube so that I would be walking back to the car warehouse about the same time that I previously would have returned from my afternoon stroll. I would then do a lap of that building before doing a lap of the motorcycle parts warehouse and returning to the car building in time to sit around waiting to clock off.

If this was Pokémon, the monster was now fully developed. In outline the day looked like this: clock in; conduct a circuit of the car parts warehouse; snooze on hidden car seat; walk over to and around the motorcycle warehouse; double-clock card; catch train to West Kensington; cook and eat lunch; watch TV and drink tea; catch train back to Gunnersbury; stroll back to the car parts warehouse; do a lap of the car parts distribution building; walk over to the motorcycle parts warehouse and do a circuit there; walk back to the car parts warehouse; clock-out; and ride back in the van to Earls Court. The alert reader will notice that there is no time in this schedule for the putting away of car or motorcycle parts.

Incredibly, this final, fully developed, phase lasted for about two weeks. The pile of un-returned parts was growing but I couldn't do anything about it; my day was full. One morning at about half-ten, I was lying on the hidden car seat when an announcement came over the PA: 'Paddy Jacaranda report to the office. Paddy Jacaranda report to the office immediately'. And so on. I climbed off the Prelude bench seat and out of the rest facility and then I walked downstairs to the open area in front of the offices where the manager was waiting. He asked me what I had been doing and I said that I had been sitting upstairs. He said that I was sacked and ordered me to leave the building.

I was more surprised than shocked. I hadn't really thought about it but I knew that something like this was coming. I walked outside and started to head towards the tube station. While it was winter it was a lovely sunny day. I had not seen the area between Cheswick and West Kens' except from the train and the van, and I had nothing else planned for the rest of that day, so I walked home. It was one of the most pleasant and liberating walks of my whole life. I enjoyed every moment as I took in the sun, and the different locations. Even the signs with the street names delighted me as I sauntered along.

Extraman was less than delighted. I was excommunicated permanently. I needed a new job and a new agency.

The Electric Ballroom

The Honda misadventure was followed by a period of limited work dominated by pubs, alcohol, pot and rock bands. I saw many innovative and exciting bands in London and I went to a lot of good venues. When I first lived in West Kens' I was a regular at the Nashville on West Cromwell and Mile End Roads. The Nashville had hosted some iconic punk bands, including the Sex Pistols and the Stranglers, but that era and the venue were on the wane. That didn't stop my continual search.

Of all the acts that I saw in London, possibly the show that I found the most powerful was Lou Reed at the Hammersmith Odeon. The Odeon was a cinema and that meant that everyone in the crowd was stuck in their seats, or more or less in that location as the crowd was on its feet. The containment added an element of frustration to the anger, energy and excitement.

The tension was intense and palpable at the end of the show when little by little the crowd forced its way across Talgarth Road. Talgarth Road was a major street with several lanes, all in one direction, and the traffic was quite heavy, but the crowd swelled out of the Odeon and surged toward Hammersmith Station, with countless individuals making their own small but significant advances, gradually blocking one lane and then the next. Once the street was bridged, the mass of hyper-excited fans surged across while the cars and lorries banked up.

Another really memorable show was Siouxsie and the Banshees at the Hammersmith Palais. Siouxsie Sioux was a great performer and once again there was a tremendous energy and excitement but at her shows the dominant colours were black and indigo-violet. The Palais' variety of spaces and engagements made it an excellent site to watch bands; you could throb in the mosh pit, hang at the edge of the action, or cast your cold critical eye over the whole affair from the upstairs lounge.

While I was still living in Avonmore Road, for several months my favourite venue was the Electric Ballroom in Camden Town. I saw many good bands there as they usually had three or four on the card with a semi-major headline act. One of the most notable of these was the Gang of Four, who I saw on the advice of Tim, my friend from the lorry unloading job.

The things that I really remember much more than the performances of the bands at the Electric Ballroom, however, were the sparse, almost vacant, dub that was sometimes played between the acts and the wonderful fashions of the young post-punkettes. At that time the building in Camden High Street was only the Electric Ballroom once every second week. These post-punk/new wave fashions were evolving rapidly and because there were different bands every fortnight there were new mixes of young women's fashions each time, just as those fashions were transforming at an incredible rate. One week there were a dozen or so young post-punkettes who had multicoloured fans of heavily-jelled and brightly-dyed hair. The fans were like sideways Mohawks or cockies' crests. I thought them, and their wearers, fantastic.

Larry turns up

During this period of venues, substances and bands following my Honda misadventure, I was largely ignoring social mores and I would get around in whatever attire came to hand. This often meant that I would appear in unusual combinations of clothes.

Just at this time a good friend from Burra arrived in London. Larry and I had planned to travel to India before he crashed his brother's uninsured car but a few months after I got there he turned up in London. I remember that first day — fresh as he was from the mid north of South Australia — more than once grabbing him and pulling him back as he was about to step in front of the traffic while he excitedly spoke to me. I'm not sure how many times this happened but the most memorable instance had him about to launch blindly into the three lanes of traffic on Warwick Road as we walked towards Earls Court before, I took hold of his shoulder.

Soon after he arrived in London, I accompanied Larry as he went over to Collingham Road to check out some potential digs. The house was run by an Australian who had been in London for a few years and, to my mind, had decided the best way to get by in the challenging foreign environment was to prey on his fellow countrymen and women. The 'landlord' had installed more panelling in the house, sort of subdividing it so he could rent out more rooms. The room being offered to Larry was actually the newly installed mezzanine in the entrance hall. Larry would have been living in this narrow, low, 'room' immediately over his arriving and departing housemates.

I'm usually quite timid but I went off. I must have been a sight because I was wearing shin-high brown boots, blue and while track pants, a tee shirt and a lumber jacket as I gave the potential landlord a piece of my mind. Larry then moved into Neil's room in our West Kens' flat; the other bed having recently been vacated by Barbara.

Larry settled right in and soon set about spreading his entertaining influence. He's an extremely funny bloke and well versed in the art of charming young women with his attentions and unlikely stories. One evening in the Kings Head I turned around to where Larry was chatting with two young Aussie girls. He was telling them that he was an air traffic controller and they were completely roped in. I believe his last full time job had been sharpening drill bits for mining equipment.

Aberdeen

Looking for cash and adventure, Larry and I set out for Aberdeen planning to get jobs as roustabouts on oil rigs in the North Sea. We had been told that prospective workers just walked from company to company until a job came up and that is what we were going to do.

Starting out from West Kensington, we used public transport and shank's pony to get out to the beginning of the M1 in view of White City. I had been past this surreal spot many times in vans going to and from casual jobs and had always found it strangely fascinating. Since the events recounted here, the site has become even more interesting for me as I think it may be the scene of the action in J G Ballard's great little novel *Concrete Island*.

After a series of rides we found ourselves in welcoming Edinburgh with its lovely, helpful, citizens. They made a great contrast to the people in London. It's not that I disliked the people in the English capital but they were very different. Londoners tended to be much more reserved, and if a tourist asked directions they might be told anything, anything that would have them moving right along, but the inhabitants of the Scottish capital, at least the ones we met, could not have been more helpful.

From Edinburgh we caught a bus to Glasgow. Getting out in the centre of the great Scottish city was a shock. Coming from

Australia, Larry and I were used to large growing cities. We had obviously spent some time in London, which did have its parts needing renewal, but the centre of Glasgow was something else. Not only were there many large derelict buildings in various states of decay, but also there were whole blocks of rubble.

Numerous drunks wandered the streets and there were more than ample drinking facilities. Burra is only a town these days but in its day it had a lot of hotels, and some old parts of Australian cities such as Sydney and Melbourne seemingly had pubs on every corner. Downtown Glasgow, however, appeared to have a saloon in the middle of every city block as well. This was Friday evening and its bars were full and loud. Most of the conversations, but not all, were happy and full of laughs.

We walked through, taking in the sights, tempted to chance one of the pubs or saloons but a little hesitant to do so. As we walked near the famous football ground of Hampden Park two boys about ten years old fired shanghais at us from the other side of the road. Shortly after that, a friendly, pleasantly intoxicated local emerged from a bar, spotted Larry and I with our backpacks, and told us to get out of there. He insisted it would be best if we got on the next bus, which we did. The bus driver gave us a bit of a quizzical look but took our fare. He then proceeded to drive the few hundred metres to the next stop, where the bus terminated.

We walked on, hitching now as we seemed to be outside the city centre, and eventually got a ride. The series of lifts that night and the next day that took us to Aberdeen were largely uneventful apart from the lift by Maureen in the Alfa Romeo that briefly had us hurtling through picturesque dales between Perth and Dundee.

I had been told that Aberdeen's old buildings are made of granite, so that their edges appear as crisp as they were the day that they were made, and when I got there the claim seemed to be true. It makes Aberdeen a very attractive town.

We found ourselves the cheapest hostel we could near the centre of the city and checked in. Monday morning we got straight into the routine that we hoped would produce well-paid jobs for us on the North Sea oil rigs. After a basic cereal-based breakfast we acquired a list of the drilling companies and a map of Aberdeen. Then we set out to visit the half dozen potential employers every morning and afternoon until we got the jobs.

One major distraction was the young women or girls of Aberdeen. Every morning as we made our way from the hostel the young office workers and senior schoolgirls would be on their way to work or to school. Then in the afternoon returning from our daily search, these same beauties, or ones like them, would also be on their homeward journeys.

Where we came from there was no shortage of people with Celtic genes honed in the British Isles. Their complexions, however, were quickly tarnished by the harsh sun. Redheads suffered the most and their delicate skin was often heavily freckled. In Aderdeen, however, these completions were common, beautiful and pristine. The translucent cheeks revealed the healthy circulation beneath. We appreciated the sights, but we carried on looking for work. Larry, of course, could not help but attract girls' attentions with his witty remarks and silly expressions.

There was something topsy turvy in the appearance of the young women insofar as the ones that were the most stunning in Aberdeen were the very ones that were the most damaged in Australia. Another carnivalesque element in Aberdeen at that time was the pubs. The hotels were warm and friendly enough but this was early summer and the traditional cry of 'Time gentlemen please' would have us walking back to the hostel in broad daylight. That did not feel right.

We religiously followed our daily routine of morning and afternoon rounds of the companies, followed by evening drinks, for a week. Then I got sick. I don't know what the problem was but I vomited and was bed ridden.

While I had my few days lying at the hostel, Larry carried on looking for work. I guess that the daily walks were less fun by yourself and by the time I had recovered, Larry's enthusiasm was waning.

The next day we had a series of friendly exchanges with two young Aussies who had recently moved into the hostel. Cheryl and Belinda had a car and they said that they were going to drive to Inverell, so we joined them. The following day they drove on to Fort William but then they decided that we were surplus to requirements, and headed off on their own.

Inverell was a really charming place and I recall seeing someone fly fishing in the river while other older men went out in their finery, including kilts. Fort William was less appealing but a couple of incidents stick in my mind.

The hostel where we stayed had several young Americans as guests. When they discovered that Ben Nevis, which is nearby, was the highest peak in Scotland, they just had to walk up it. We lounged around town instead, and chatted to a couple of young locals. As we did two young men came along in their ridiculous pants. One of the locals commented that you could tell the Americans by their tartan trousers.

That evening when we went to a hotel it was full. The Scottish FA Cup was on; the Old Firm, as they say. The crowd in the hotel was glued to the screen and the barracking was intense. Eventually, Celtic scored. Half the crowd were extremely excited and several people actually jumped onto tables or chairs. You wouldn't look sideways at the other half of the patrons, who presumably were rooting for Rangers.

Hitching back to London a young French couple on their honeymoon picked us up and insisted that they give us lunch. This generous pair were camped in a little van on the side of Loch Ness; a secluded spot with a very pleasant view. Lunch was basic in the French way that people often forget when they focus instead on Parisian sauces: chips, boiled eggs, quartered tomatoes and boiled white rice with a little salad dressing; delicious. As for the couple, you could only hope their lives together were long and happy.

Continuing south with whoever would give us a lift, we found ourselves travelling through some drought-ravaged dales north of the English border. Everything is relative, so a few weeks without rain was normal for us but in this part of Scotland it was no joke. Disaster was looming as the water storages were only made to carry about a month's supply, and the whole place was so dry that we were actually driven through a grass fire in the rolling hills and moorland of the Scottish Borders district.

The last ride back to London was in a lorry that appeared to be designed to haul some kind of heavy bulk material and it seemed to be returning empty. The driver batted away our questions about the cargo with nonsense claims including that he was carrying weighted glider engines.

Tusselix, self, and other destructions

The rise of methamphetamine has brought the cough medicines containing pseudoephedrine to the fore, and to the attention of the popular press, but in the time of yore, that is, prior to the first time someone showed a bikie how to make meth' out of the stuff, these medicines were appreciated in their natural, raw condition. Even then some concoctions were more highly-prized than others and many of these were prescription drugs. Several that I knew of, however, were available from chemists. One of these was Tusselix Forte.

I think I had Tusselix only once in Adelaide and then I was probably semi-controlled; by which I mean I believe I only had about four times the recommended dose.

One day in London, however, Larry and I found ourselves at a party in a place just off Warwick Road to the west of Earls Court. The little terrace was completely full and we were crammed into a little hall next to the kitchen when someone unearthed an enormous bottle of Tusselix Forte. It was probably only half a litre but it seemed like a king brown. After a brief discussion about the virtues of the bottle's contents, we started sampling it. Four of us ended up drinking the bottle in short order and then the fun began. We carried on like loose tappets for the rest of the party. Then we ran — yes ran — home to West Kens' in synchronised jogging.

The footpath on the West Cromwell Road bridge over the railway lines between Earls Court and West Kensington had a brick or concrete wall along its edge. Not for the first time, I walked along the top of the wall, looking down as I did onto the tracks many metres below with the deluded self-confidence that stimulants can instil. At another point in our manic journey — or was it another night, I can't be entirely sure — I took time out to scratch a sports car. Larry was rightly disgusted. Soon after that he headed off for his own adventures in Germany.

PART 2

Where did all the money go?

There are two clear facts and there is a lot of murkiness in between. When I first got to London I had thousands of dollars. I'm not sure of the exact amount but must have been about £4000. In less than a year it was all gone, and the great majority of it was gone in six months.

I'm reminded of George Best's statement: 'I spent a lot of my money on booze, birds and fast cars — the rest I just squandered'. The truth, however, is far less glamorous largely because I'm not much of a womaniser, never having had much confidence in that department. Accommodation, alcohol, watching rock bands, and substance abuse would have accounted for a lot of my disposed income. A significant chunk, however, was truly wasted.

What I do know is where an amount approaching £300 went. It went to a great big drunken Scottish scaffolder and a couple of his mates. I don't remember exactly how I started to lend Jimmy the money but I do know how hard it was to stop. It would have begun in one of the pubs around Earls Court. I would have been drunk, full of artificial and exaggerated confidence, and inflated good will. I suppose I found out he needed some money and generously, foolishly, naively, gave him some. Then, as the relationship rapidly developed — it was a relationship insofar as he kept finding me, and increasingly obviously — it became a little like those Nigerian Internet scams because there was always some reason why it was in my best interest to tide him over until he got his outstanding money from a job.

Jimmy really was a scaffolder, and so were the couple of mates of his, who were both also Scottish; they had actually done scaffolding. In recent times, however, they spent more time between jobs than in them and more waking hours in the pub than elsewhere, when they had the money and it was mine that they were drinking now. Between the alcohol and the pot, happenstance and cunning deviousness manufacturing both need and its antidote, there was a slow turning of consciousness to working out how to get out of the situation.

That need, which was already dawning on me, became blindingly obvious when Jimmy turned up first thing one morning with a continuation of his story. Not even fully awake I went off with him and one of his big mates was there. This financial exchange was right on the cusp of lending and being robbed because they were both big and threatening. It would be hard to prove in court that I had been unwillingly violated but the menace was tangible.

The worm had to turn and the next day I hunted around the Earls Court pubs until I found Jimmy. Fortunately I found him by himself and not with one or other of those other large, hairy lumps. I told Jimmy that the situation had become ridiculous and there was no sign of the promised money from the yet-to-be-paid scaffolding job. I told him that he and his mates owed me nearly three hundred pounds and I said something would have to be done about it. Jimmy didn't deny that he owed the money but nor did he say he would get it. Things were now out in the open and he abused and threatened me and then left. I should, I suppose have gone to police then, although I don't think I could have proven anything but my own foolishness. Still, it's almost certain that Jimmy would have had some kind of form.

That really was the end because Jimmy and co. disappeared. He no longer turned up at whatever pub I was drinking. I don't know that I did anything approaching another search for the stinking, soaking, scaffolders but I didn't need to because I was frequenting most of the pubs in the area and I didn't see them again. Well, that might not be quite right. One night on Earls Court Road I did see a large dark hairy figure on the other side of the road, hastening south. It might have been Jimmy but I'm not sure.

The lovely people at
the Information Distribution Office

Over-generosity, lack of work, laziness, watching bands, drinking and taking drugs all eventually took their toll. As well as being increasingly poor, I had also become a bit of a physical wreck. Luckily, just as an early decrepitude loomed I got a job at a government facility at Brook Green, near Hammersmith, called the Information Distribution Office, or some such thing. I'll call it the IDO.

I was given the job by one of the agencies around Earls Court — obviously not Extraman, which had given me a lifetime ban — but one further up Earls Court Road in the direction of Kensington Road and Holland Park. The job was not wanted by the expats who made up the agency's casual wage slaves because it paid for an hour less each day than virtually every other job on their list.

The IDO, however, suited me perfectly. It was just what I needed at the time. This small marvel of the British public service distributed newspapers and news journals to the British embassies and consulates in all quarters of the globe. There were a series of deadlines — three or four during the day — and we would ready all the sets of newspapers and magazines for the embassies and consulates in the relevant parts of the world. So, for example, the first deadline each day might have been for the British Government representatives in the Americas and south and west Africa, and we would have packed up all their newspapers and journals well before that deadline and then settled down for a while. A few of the workers sat around chatting but several of us used to take the opportunity and read some of the plentiful materials around us.

When I say 'take the opportunity', I should point out how much opportunity there was. While we were only paid for seven hours, and that, apparently, is what made the job undesirable for expat-working-holidaymakers, I calculated that once you took out lunch and the morning and afternoon tea breaks, there was a maximum of five hours and twenty minutes of potential work time. The time actually needed to get the newspapers and magazines all packed up for the series of deadlines, however, it took about half of that so there was plenty left over to read and there was everything a budding British information junkie could wish for. I regularly browsed a variety of newspapers and news magazines including the *Spectator*, but every day I read the *Guardian* and the *Times*. Funnily enough, my favourite was the *Times*.

The tabloids were completely unpalatable. They didn't devote much attention to the things I was most interested in, mainly international politics, and I got sick of the constant stream of cartoons depicting Arthur Scargill as a dragon with Margaret Thatcher as St George. I would have thought the irony of those images was obvious but the variations on the theme appeared were both very limited and endless.

I was the only casual at the IDO and I must have been a sight to begin with. Apart from the manager and me, all of the workers were older. The women felt sorry for me and mothered me, and all of them were very generous. One old Indian chap brought in some slipper-like shoes, which I then wore for the next month or so. I can't remember the footwear I had when I first turned up to work at the IDO but it must have been glaringly obvious to all that it was somehow deficient.

The manager clearly had some personal issues. After hiding in her office all morning, she would appear not long after lunch for her lap of the works; swanning around in an airy, vague, and overly friendly way. I found this daily performance completely inoffensive. It was certainly better than having a boss stand over you. My fellow workers told me that the manager had some relationship problems, she was very anxious and she was taking Valium, and all of that was consistent with what I saw, which very much reminded me of *Morning Becomes Electra*.

All good things must come to pass and after a few weeks at the IDO I was no longer needed; someone was returning or they had a permanent replacement or something like that. I was sad to leave but I was much, much, healthier, I had a few pounds and I was leaving in my comfortable slippers.

The departures of Warren and Neil

Almost as soon as I finished my job at the IDO, my flat mates Neil and Warren decided they would both go back to Australia via India. Warren's plans were simple, well organised and properly financed, but Neil's were more flexible and ambitious.

Warren bought a ticket to Melbourne that included a three-month stopover in Bombay. That would allow him to travel as far as he liked in India but with relative security.

Neil was still in no great hurry to return to Australia and he had less money than Warren. Naturally, he came up with an outrageously optimistic plan. Neil bought a ticket to Delhi and another from Bombay to Perth, Western Australia. The second flight would leave Bombay many months after he arrived in Delhi. Neil intended to travel overland using his very limited monetary resources but much greater charm and guile.

In the event, the contrasts between Neil and Warren's departures were even starker. After a quiet evening featuring just a few bongs with a couple of friends from East Gippsland, the next morning Warren headed off to the tube stop, never to be seen by me again.

The night before Neil's flight to Delhi we had a huge session at the Kings Head where numerous friends bought him even more drinks. Heavily hung over the next morning, Neil headed off to Heathrow just in time to miss his flight. Luckily, he was put on the same flight the following day and he managed to catch it. He had £5 on which he was to survive for more than six months as he made his way from Delhi to Bombay, including a planned side trip to Kashmir.

Stan Trout and the Corner House

As Neil and Warren made their plans to vacate Avonmore Road, I should have organised some new accommodation but for one reason or another I hadn't got around to it. This was especially foolish given that the expiry of the lease had been arranged and the bond was going to Warren.

Suddenly, if foreseeably, homeless, I started a thirteenth hour search for new accommodation. In Earls Court I ran into Stan Trout. Trout was a one off. He was from Mooloolaba on Queensland's Sunshine Coast; or the North Coast as he still called it. Trout had arrived in London bearing his surfboard and fifty kangaroo hides, which he sold. Trout loved to laugh and he loved to drink and he was a real action figure. Some thought him childish and found his laughing annoying, but I saw something wonderfully genuine and real in Trout.

Trout's financial plummet in London had been even more spectacular than my own. He laughingly used to tell the story of how at one point he got down to having only a single set of footwear and that was a pair of wellies. For some reason, one rainy morning when he was beginning a new job on a building site, he found that the wellies were the only footwear he still had, so he had ridden on the tube and done his job in these for that whole first week. Presumably part of his first pay went on getting a decent set of work boots.

I had known Trout for a couple of months but when I ran into him this day it happened that he had just managed to have himself evicted. Finding ourselves both digs-free we set out to secure some kind of home, and we did so by going to the pub. This led us to the Corner House, and our relationship with it was strange and complex right from the start.

That night we were chatting to some South Africans at the Kings Head. These guys were rig workers who spent most of their time somewhere between the north of Scotland and Denmark but they maintained a flat in London for their time off.

There was a spare bed or lounge or something back there and we were welcome to it. The instructions were interesting. First, they said, you could open the lock in the building's front door with a half-p coin. Then you went up to the second floor where their flat was the first one hard right. They didn't have a spare key but informed us that a little shove was all that was needed to access the flat. We had no drinking money left so we headed off to the corner of Warwick Road and Philbeach Gardens, which is where the Corner House was.

The first part of the plan was easy and required very little gumption. We had the requisite coin and we were soon inside and up the stairs. There was a nervous moment, however, outside the door that we presumed to be that of the South Africans' before we entered the flat because we didn't want to get the attention of the neighbours by knocking but, bearing in mind that we had never been in the building before and were not entirely sure that this was the right room, or even that the guys at the pub hadn't been pulling our legs, we were fearful of busting in on some unsuspecting residents. Biting the bullet we gave the door a quick hard shove and were inside. No problem.

We helped ourselves to some tea and waited for the rig workers. After the pub shut they turned up with a few beers. They gave us a beer each while they drank and smoked some heroin. They must have been loaded because they even gave us a little smoke. That was enough to send me to the land of nod till morning.

Michelle and the Warwick Road hostel

The next night at the Kings Head, I ran into Michelle. Michelle was the girlfriend of Pat, the Kiwi wool-classer-come-substance-distributer who had been so rude and then so generous at our Avonmore Road party. Michelle was getting very friendly and told me that she and Pat were off. She said that Pat had gone to France and might not be back. This did not quite jell with the other reports that I had heard which were basically along the lines that Pat was gone for a couple of weeks on a holiday or business venture. The other stories also made no mention of Pat and Michelle being off.

By the time the pub was shutting, Michelle and I were getting very cosy. It turned out, however, that she was also between homes. When we hit the street outside she was wrapped hard against my side as she told me about a hostel on Warwick Road where it might be possible to sneak in for the night.

When we got down to Warwick Road Michelle directed me along the side of a building into the gardens behind. From there it was easy to climb a fence and force the back door of the hostel. Inside the hostel's rear entrance was a room with a sink, a lounge and some boxes of stored materials. We cuddled up on the lounge where we managed to make love and then sleep in a quite limited space; we were both pretty skinny at the time.

The whole experience was pleasant but not quite as pleasant as might be imagined because while we were actually having sex on the lounge Michelle complained that Pat wouldn't have just forced the rear door. Pat, said Michelle, while we are at it, would have climbed around the side of the building, through the window and into the last guest room where there was a double bed.

When we had finished, I asked how Pat would know that there weren't any guests in there. Michelle replied that it was the least booked room and whenever Pat had forced his way in there it was always vacant. There was a tone about this that fell well short of new found love.

Rising to the challenge, the next night I ran into Michelle again and without too much ado we left together at the end and went straight down to Warwick Road. This time I worked up the seemingly-required gumption and climbed up to the window of the last guest room in the hostel. It was fairly easy to slip the catch and soon we were both in.

This cosy little arrangement lasted for about five or six nights. The next night, however, I more or less anticipated running into Michelle again but she didn't appear. I found out later that she had a new temporary friend and that seemed to keep her going until Pat's return, when it transpired that they had not been off at all, and Pat was less than happy with the reports he heard of Michelle's extracurricular activities.

The first evening that Michelle didn't materialise at the Kings Head, I was still without accommodation, so I went by myself to the hostel. When I had made my way to the garden behind the hostel I could see that the light was on in the back bedroom. As I crept closer, I could hear voices so I simply and quietly forced the back door as I had done on the first night with Michelle. The room had been rearranged and boxes were stacked onto the lounge. There also appeared to be a changed lock on the door that connected the room to the rest of the house.

I took the boxes off the lounge and lay down for the night. It seemed clear to me that someone in the hostel had worked out the back room had been used. The replacement of the lock was consistent with a suspicion that someone had come into the back room from the front, possibly let in by one of the guests. So I stacked the boxes next to the door to give me some time if there were any sudden interruptions.

Camping on the roof

As soon as I woke up the next morning in the rear room of the Warwick Road hostel, I put the boxes back onto the lounge before I snuck out the rear entrance. I felt sure that someone was onto the situation and would realise that a person had slept there so I was very determined to find another venue and not return to the hostel for the foreseeable future.

That afternoon I ran into Trout again. Once again he was also looking for somewhere to stay and he came up with a novel temporary solution to our diminished circumstances.

Next to the bathroom that we had used in the Corner House was a ladder way leading to the roof of the building. Trout suggested that we haul our belongings up there until we could find somewhere to stay. Being, as we were at the time, in a groove of extreme apathy and indifference, we didn't get around to finding alternative accommodation that day, or the next, or the next... That's how we came to live on the roof of the Corner House.

After a couple of days we were set up on the roof. We had a mattress, a couple of sleeping bags, a couple of cushions, and a little butane cooker of the sort you might use for a picnic on a day trip to the country. The soft furnishings had been recycled from neighbourhood skips but I've got no idea where the little gas burner and fry pan came from; they must have been Trout's.

This was a magical London summer. It must have been a drought by the English capital's standards and while we ended up camping on the roof of the Corner House for several weeks, maybe even more than a month, we were extremely lucky as it only rained a few times.

When it did rain we simply picked up the mattress and the other belongings that needed to be protected, and jumped over onto the roof next door. There we would climb down a ladder to the second floor where we would set up on the bare floorboards. The whole building was just a shell with only the timber inside. It had been stripped back to the timber because it was being refurnished.

One afternoon when it was drizzling, we were next door in the vacant building lying on the mattress looking out through the two empty window frames. The view outside was nondescript, mainly grey sky with just the very tops of the buildings directly across Warwick Road. 'What's out that window?' I said to Trout. 'India', he replied. 'What's out that one?' 'South America', he said. We both laughed.

When you share a moment like that it is tempting to think that you share the same thought but that might not be true. I don't know what Trout was thinking because after we finished laughing we just went on to something else. Even so, I know what I was thinking and I suspect that Trout was thinking something similar. It seemed that our circle of acquaintances, many of who had little money, were always moaning and most claimed that they were going to travel somewhere. In these conversations the popular destinations were South America and India. Now, when we laughed it was as if we both knew that we weren't going anywhere. That's what I thought anyway, but I can't be sure if that was in Trout's mind.

One time when the drizzle had driven us next door we must have dozed off and slept through the night because then next thing we knew we were being woken by a young apprentice builder or labourer telling us to move off smartly as the boss was about to come up. So we quickly gathered up our things and headed back over onto the roof of the Corner House.

It was unbelievably idyllic up there on the roof of the Corner House. Day and night we laughed about our luck and the oddity of it — two Aussies camping out on a roof in the middle of London. We were certainly blessed weather-wise but that wasn't the only way that we were riding our luck.

There was a small supermarket in Earls Court that appeared to be monitored by an elaborate security camera system. On closer inspection, however, I realised that there was only one operational camera and it faced toward the front of the store. All the other lenses were inoperative simulations designed to give the impression that every corner of the shop was under surveillance. The meat section was at the back of the shop and I got into the habit of stealing steaks.

Then, while Trout and I were camped on the roof of the Corner House, he got a job labouring for a contractor who seemed to get work digging trenches and the like. We established a routine where Trout would bring back some kind of vegetable matter in the afternoon when he returned from his job and I would get the meat. What this meant was that my frequent stealing from the supermarket became the daily theft of a two-pack of steaks.

My method was always the same. I would walk into the shop and wander around as if looking for something but really checking out where the staff were. Then I would walk to the back of the shop, choose the pack, have one quick last look around and slip the pack under my coat. When I was doing the steak stealing on a casual basis I would sometimes then just stroll out of the supermarket. However, I thought that would be too suspicious when I was going into the shop every day so when I was taking the steak two-packs I would have to buy some very small and inexpensive item. Often, this would be a small tub of yoghurt.

Once you are in this kind of routine you don't normally spend a lot of time considering its morality. If you did I think you would have to stop, or try to. I usually did not judge the action;

I was concentrating on doing it without being caught. One day, however, an employee cut through that veneer. I was lined up with the small yoghurt in my hand and the steaks under my coat when one of the young Indians or Pakistanis who worked in the shop said hello. That made me feel like a complete heel and now when I look back I'm ashamed not only of the theft but in the way that it turned the staff into objects to be feared instead of human beings.

A few days after that piercing greeting, Trout and I were sitting on the roof. It was a gorgeous summery afternoon and we were sharing a little joint and chatting away when, suddenly, the trap door shot up and some police emerged. To me it was like cybermen had terrifyingly invaded and destroyed our momentary urban idyll. Trout had the presence of mind to flick the roach of the joint over the side of the building but the police caught a glimpse of his action which just meant that they searched him more thoroughly than they would have, and quickly found the little bit of hash that he had on him.

It was a strange little scene up there on the roof of the Corner House. The police didn't take long to ascertain the extent of our domain and possessions. We were hardly asked any questions and then we were told to collect our things. All that we had, except the mattress, was wrapped up into a sheet and hauled along as we were escorted downstairs.

Kensington Police Station

Soon enough we found ourselves in the Kensington Police Station. I was put into a cell with another young bloke while Stan Trout was put into another cell by himself. This was my first police cell experience and I was on a steep learning curve. The cell had two hard benches attached to the side walls. The outside wall had a high window made of thick heavily frosted glass that allowed you to see whether it was day or night, but that was about it. Directly opposite was the steel door which also had a small window in it at about head height. On the other side of the window, however, was a little door that filled in the whole space of the window apart from a couple of millimetres of clearance through which it was possible to peek into the police station proper.

I was basically locked up and forgotten about. That was because I was not the one with the little bit of pot and nor was I the suspect in the much larger crime that was the main concern to the police.

The other guy in my cell, Geoff, was a doorman for some dodgy club somewhere between Kensington High Street and West Cromwell Road. He had been picked up for a driving offence. The police had taken a urine sample and one came along and gave him another container to fill up. He asked me if I'd had anything alcoholic to drink that day and I said I hadn't but warned him that I'd smoked some hash. Geoff wasn't worried about that and asked me to provide the sample. I did my best but I was nervous and hadn't had a drink of recent times and only managed to provide a very marginal sample. I'm not sure if it did the trick or not because when I ran into him a couple of weeks later, which is the only other time I ever saw him, the police were still considering their options with the two very different samples.

Inmates of the police cells were allowed to smoke but not to have lighters or matches. There was a button that the prisoners could use to call for service such as asking for a light but ringing it was a complete waste of time because nothing happened. Furthermore, the button for the barely-audible bell was very hard to press and pressing it quickly hurt your finger or thumb. This made the room service arrangement a test of endurance. You had to really want something and have the strength to ring long enough to annoy the police sufficiently for them to do something about it.

After several hours of incarceration a policeman came into the cell and gave us a Styrofoam cup of tea. The tea was cool and weak but the visit gave us a chance to ask for a light. The kindly young copper obliged. From then on, for the next few hours until Geoff was let out we chain-smoked; one lighting his cigarette off the butt of the other's smoke.

By the time Geoff was gone it was evening. There only seemed to be one policeman around and that was the desk sergeant. He was a large, dark haired, round-faced bloke in his late thirties. He had nothing better to do than to ignore the occasional faint buzzing from one or other of the captives while he sat at his desk reading.

As evening turned to night two policemen came in with a distressed young woman. I could hear as they sat her down and gave her a cup of tea. I don't know what she had done but it was clear that the two who brought her in had done so on the understanding that she was suicidal. They questioned her and tried to calm her down. Eventually they left leaving her sitting quietly on a kind of bench seat that was a few metres behind the chair of the desk sergeant. I could see the seat through the bottom left hand corner edge of the window in the door of my cell.

Not long after the other two police had gone the sergeant got up and went over and started talking to the young woman. I couldn't hear what he was saying but I could hear the increasingly loud and adamant denials of the young woman. I think he was accusing her of faking it. This action attracted my attention so I got up again and started watching through the edge of my window. As their discussion went on, the sergeant sat down on the bench seat on the far side of the women. She was wearing a striped long sleeved top seemingly made out of a stretchy T-shirt material. The young woman was quite solid without being fat and had large bosoms. She was also wearing a bra as I soon saw because the sergeant continued in his goading tone and started to learn over her as he sat next to her before he shoved his hand down her top. He was still making that horrible accusative kind of sound as he had his hand inside her bra. I could clearly see him groping her breast. I was shocked and appalled. I was thinking, 'She's in here because she is extremely distressed and you're doing that'.

Perhaps I made a sound or maybe the policeman just realised that he could be seen from my cell. He got up looking in my direction and headed straight to my window where he violently jerked open the little door. Seeing him coming I quickly sat down. My bum was barely hitting the bench when the window shot open and he looked in. I tried to give a look of ignorance mixed with apathy. He stared at me suspiciously before slamming the window shut again. I waited until I could hear him back on the bench talking to the woman again before I resumed my place at the window. Once again he had her by the breast and was leaning over her. Then he seemed to hear something else and he got up and returned to his seat and that's where he was sitting a few minutes later when one of the two policemen who had brought in the girl reappeared. Soon after that the distressed young lady was taken away and I never saw her again.

While all this was going on, Trout was leading a much more interesting life, insofar as he had been taken in and out of his cell a couple of times for interviews. Not that I knew it, because I couldn't see his cell and I had been told nothing.

Sometimes you have to really wonder about people's suspicions and how they can put one and one together and get five. Apparently, there was a serial and successful cat burglar operating in Chelsea. We weren't far from Chelsea. Cat burglars climb onto roofs. We were on a roof. We could be cat burglars. I guess the reasoning went something like that. Why Trout was suspected and not me I don't know. He was taller and had fair hair and maybe those features better fit whatever description the police had of the cat burglar.

As I found out later, we were being held until the next day so some detective covering the Chelsea cat burglar case could come and interview Trout. I've heard many stories where people are suspected of some much greater crime and then when the investigator realises that they have been disappointed the suspect gets let off the lesser crime and this looked like being another one of those cases. When the detective turned up late the next morning he didn't take long to realise that the Queensland Warwick Road roof camper and the Chelsea cat burglar were not one and the same. The detective felt his time and effort had been wasted. Urban roof camping really falls more in the unusual category than the seriously criminal so that only left the matter of the very small amount of hash that Trout was arrested with. All the Chelsea detective could promise on that front was that if it turned out to be less than a gram they would let him off. It eventually came in at just under one gram and the whole thing was forgotten.

As soon as the detective headed back to Chelsea, Trout and I were let out of our cells. It was twenty-four hours since those black and blue cybermen emerged onto the roof of the Corner House and I had been given one dishwater cup of tea and nothing to eat; I would remember that.

We were given back our possessions and told to go. Looking like a hilariously grotesque parody of Huckleberry Finn with all our possessions wrapped in a sheet, we headed out the door. As we were leaving one of the police asked where we were going to go. We stopped, looked, thought, and said the Kings Head. They just shook their heads as we walked off.

Bramham Gardens revisited

When we got down to the Kings Head, Trout started trying to chase up old friends and colleagues that he might stay with while I also turned my mind to the problem of accommodation.

I thought of the building that I used to visit the other side of Earls Court Road in Bramham Gardens. I had first gone there to a party soon after I arrived in London and then been a frequent visitor. At that time it was full of colonials, mainly Australians and South Africans. One way or another, an ex-pat couple ended up owning the place. As it happens, he was from South Africa and she was from my home town. The house had been a full and lively place when I went there for casual post-pub parties, and later I went there several times to buy pot from Pat, the Kiwi former wool-classer who had moved into a less arduous profession.

The fact that the building was vacant awaiting refurbishment was hardly a secret. I might even have gone to the closing down party. I knew the place would be empty for at least a little while. So I went around to Bramham Gardens and investigated the house with a view to finding a way in so I could have somewhere to stay. At the front of the building the view over the gardens was very pleasant. Like many of these so-called gardens in London, there was a rectangular park surrounded by streets of joined three or four story buildings, all nice and white.

The building had been well boarded up and I could not get in without making a lot of noise and doing some obvious damage.

After some time trying to gain entry via the relatively open and exposed front of the house I decided that getting in that way wasn't an option.

When I went around the back, however, the story was very different. Where the front was a pastoral of white and green, the lane behind the building was then a more grey fugue. Hesper Mews was a quiet, discrete, little street and separating the rear of the property from it was an old brick wall about six feet high with a flat top, one brick length thick.

I pulled myself up so I could see over the wall. The small area behind the building, about three meters squared, was richly grassed and slightly higher than the level of the lane, so jumping over the wall involved a little less impact than would otherwise have been the case.

Once on the welcoming grass, I tried to get in but the back door was bolted shut from the inside and the window had impenetrable bars. At the back of the building, however, there was also a small lean-to that had been either an outdoor WC or a little shed with a gently sloping roof. There was some stone or brickwork next to the lean-to that made it easier to climb onto its low roof. That gave me access to the first floor window.

The window had no bars and was only jammed shut. With a little bit of effort I was able to force it up and find my way inside. Once in there I looked around and found that the whole place was vacant, except for the rubbish left by the final occupants. There were at least four floors to enjoy but there was no point going any further than that first bedroom because none of the services were working.

As soon as I had surveyed the domain I headed back to the Kings Head. Trout was still there with all the gear wrapped up in the sheet. In his alternative accommodation search he had only had nibbles; there were no firm offers. If he didn't find anything else then some friends over the river at Putney might have been able to take him in but they hadn't committed themselves.

I told Trout about the situation at Bramham Gardens. He also knew the building and had been there. We went straight around with the gear and hauled it up through the window. There were still a lot of papers and cans lying around but I had cleared a space. There we set up our sleeping bags and some other basic recycled bedding. We cleared another space for Trout's little butane camping cooker.

The housing provided by the empty Bramham Gardens building was very much just a sleeping quarters, although the little cooker did see some service. For all other services we had to use the public facilities provided in the area, especially including those available at the Kings Head.

We spent a lot of time at the pub while we stayed at Bramham Gardens. Many's the time that we would be sitting on the step of the Kings Head, facing east down Kenway Road, waiting for the pub to open in the afternoon, or even in the morning. We would be sitting there reading our free Australian newspapers when the barmaid, Joanne, would come and open up.

Joanne sort of took us under her wing and gave us everything she could without officially giving us anything. We would come in with our free newspapers and she would give us a drink. We were welcome to any drink that was entirely made of mixers because she didn't have to account for them. So we would often get a soda with lime, or something like that, and then adjourn to the far table where we would sit reading the Australian papers.

If any colonials came in we were good for conversation and if anyone offered us a drink we wouldn't say no. The glory years of colonialdom had moved on from the Kings Head but you still got some strays in there, or others like us who were living on the fringes, though maybe not quite so on the fringes as Trout and I.

One quiet afternoon during this time we were in the Kings Head sitting at a table where two other alternative ex-pats had joined us. Also in the pub were four South Africans who we knew were doing a variety of drugs. The only other table to be occupied had a group of the pub's occasional clients, possibly English, that

Trout and I had seen smoking grass in Knaresborough Place a little earlier that day.

Into this narrow but comfortable scene came three police. The police wore plain clothes but were as plain as the nose on your face. Everyone saw immediately and acted accordingly.

Without saying a word we put down (that is, drank) our drinks and headed straight out the door onto Hogarth Place. The police had just got to the bar and hadn't even turned around to survey the pub by the time we were going out the door and the South Africans were already leaving via the Kenway Road exit.

As soon as we were outside we turned right and walked briskly but without obviously rushing. When we were about halfway to Earls Court Road I glanced behind and saw that the English pot smokers were trailing us by about 25 metres, and behind them I could see the police coming out of the door of the Kings Head. The pub had been cleared in less than thirty seconds.

The pizza runner

The first Saturday afternoon after Trout and I had made ourselves at home in Bramham Gardens we went to a party in Nevern Place, three streets down Earls Court Road from the tube station and about two hundred metres around the corner. As usual we had some alcohol from where I know not. It was a lovely warm, sunny afternoon and the drinks began to take effect.

Trout and I were talking with Phineas T. Freakears and Bluey Dunstan. Phineas T. Freakears supposedly bore that moniker because of certain resemblances to the Furry Freak Brothers cartoon character. In fact, I thought that he looked like a combination of two of the comic's characters; Phineas T. Freakears, because of his spirals of black hair, and Fat Freddy, because he was rotund. I had known him for several months; he was another local Aussie identity. When I first met Phineas T. he was living with his girlfriend in a Kombi van that was semi-permanently parked in Kenway Road, not far down from the Kings Head. They would have seemed halcyon days given his present circumstances but he still had the black steel coil hair and had managed to remain portly. Bluey was a mate of Phineas T. Freakears and I only ever met him a couple of times, including this day at the Nevern Place afternoon garden party.

Unsurprisingly, none of us had any money and the combination of that fact, the alcohol, the warm sunny afternoon, and some kind of nostalgic muse about food and runners led us to hatch a plan. The plan was simplicity itself and it went like this: the four of us would go down to the pizza shop on Earls Court Road, have some pizza, and then do a runner.

So we headed off to the pizza shop. The restaurant was almost full but we managed to get a cosy table for four only one table away from the door. Some of us had never been in the shop before, I certainly hadn't, and when we got the menu we were a little disappointed. Not to be deterred, each one of us ordered a large pizza. I think we all got supremes.

The second hiccup, after the menu, was the fact that this was in the early afternoon, non-drinking period that London had at the time…still part of the effort for the First World War. Given that we were ordering money-free, there was no point skimping on the drinks but there was little choice so all four of us ordered large glasses of milk. That was a bad decision.

The meals arrived and we began to eat. We did so very nervously as we surveyed the situation and thought about our escape. We noted that the waiter would regularly but briefly disappear into the kitchen to retrieve food or drinks for the patrons. It seemed to me that the waiter was very suspicious of us four, as he had every right to be, but this might only have been a paranoid projection… it's hard to tell.

As we considered our situation and the desirability of a quick getaway, the black steel spirals on Phineas T. Freakears' head were not an issue but his portly girth was. That handicap, or should I just say 'difference', was now one of our main concerns as we ate our pizzas, drank our milk, and eyed the waiter and the doors.

The escape plan we agreed on was succinct but it included a modicum of consideration. Once we had all finished our meals, we would sit calmly chatting until the waiter next went into the back of the restaurant. As soon as he disappeared we would get up and leave. Phineas T. would be allowed to go out the door first but then it would be every man, woman and child for themselves.

A minute or two later, the waiter went through the back door and we quickly rose and exited out the front, following Phineas T. We pushed through the door and once we hit the bitumen the race was on. We sprinted only a short distance along the footpath before shooting through the on-coming traffic to the greater safety of the other side of the road where we continued running at full speed through the pedestrians.

Even in this desperate flight there was a moment of brevity. We were local characters and it was almost inevitable that we would see and be seen by people we knew. As it happened, on Earls Court Road just down from the station we sprinted through a group of people who were making their way from the party. Pat and Michelle were part of a group of about six who laughed as we raced through them.

The waiter had briefly run after us. I think he gave up as soon as we crossed the road but he may well have been telephoning the police so there was no stopping. We sprinted back the few blocks along Earls Court Road and around the corner to the party. We couldn't wait for someone to let us in so we jumped through the window.

Puffing and panting we were all on the verge of vomiting (that milk had definitely been a mistake) but once we were in the back garden again we started to relax. Nervously and laughingly we debriefed before Trout's nostalgic mind turned to his childhood tree climbing. It was a topic dear to my own heart too so I enthusiastically chorused. As so often happened when Trout said something like that, the next thing it was realised.

I looked around and there was Trout, way up the tree, back in his youth, where he was headed again.

Foreigners and the medical centre

Another leisurely afternoon while Trout and I were squatting in Bramham Gardens, I was drinking at the Kings Head when a middle-aged Englishman started to tell me about a great, easy, well-paying job he had nearby at what he said would be a posh medical centre for Saudis. This got him onto the topic of race, not that he needed any help. As well as rich Arabs, Barry had a strong dislike of West Indians, and pretty well all people of colour. He also went on about how the Russians just stole all their technology and some other well-trodden paths, but dark-skinned people in England was his main bugbear. If he wasn't in the National Front, I would have given him a reference.

Anyway, given that I was job-free and penniless, I was interested in his lucrative employment opportunity. He gave me the address and told me to be there at nine in the morning. When I arrive it turns out that there is not exactly a job there for me. What he has in mind is more a kind of subcontracting arrangement. He must have been paid quite well, because he offers me cash for doing his job if I come there in the mornings and take his place while he goes off to the pub. The arrangement was extremely dodgy but the pay was basically the same as I would have received working through an employment agency. The job was also only a few minutes from Hesper Mews, not far the other side of Cromwell Road, so I agreed.

The glass that we were installing was about an inch thick. The other labourers told me that it was bullet proof and it was being installed around what would be operating theatres in the medical centre.

The job was usually pretty easy. For much of the time, we labourers would do nothing or very little but the actual installation of the glass was a heavy job. Personally, I suspect that Barry was beginning to feel his age and was happy to part with a significant portion of his wage to save his back, as well as to enjoy a few drinks.

About one week into this work arrangement luck intervened. Trout and I were walking home from the pub when we spotted a £10 note lying on the footpath. I immediately bend over and reached down to pick it up but was still an inch or so from the prize when the flash of Trout's hand took the note out of my grasp. It didn't make one iota of difference because we turned right around and went straight back to the Kings Head where we drank the tanner.

A few hours later we found ourselves walking back to the tradesmen's entrance of our Bramham Gardens abode. I flew over the wall in the usual manner, but instead of the comfortable landing that I had come to expect, my right foot hit something hard and my ankle exploded in excruciating pain. Hidden in the grass was an old hardwood beam and I had landed on its edge. After composing myself, I managed to climb up to our digs.

The next day I hobbled around to the building site. Barry was disappointed with my condition and he pointed out that I obviously couldn't do the job. I had to agree. Needless to say there was no talk of compensation or sickness benefits. I was incapacitated and unemployed for the remainder of my time at Bramham Gardens.

They didn't know we were staying there, but we still had friends who socialised with the owners of the building in Bramham Gardens and we knew the day was fast approaching when we would have to move out.

Tripping to Charlie's place

While Trout and I had been living on the roof of the Corner House, he had experienced a couple of weeks of one of the most difficult and ridiculous jobs imaginable. His work gang had been tunnelling to put a service under a roadway and a footpath, putting pipes in or something like that, but did not have the appropriate tools. They only had some more basic trench-making equipment including a jackhammer. So, in lieu of a large drill, one person would be in the trench operating the jackhammer horizontally while the other held it up. I did not witness this operation but Trout said that most of the time he was the one holding the jackhammer up. The way he described it to me, Trout usually stood above the jackhammer holding onto a rope that was wrapped around it just next to its chisel-like bit while his co-worker operated the machine, pushing it toward the ground they were trying to remove. You can imagine how difficult it was taking the weight of the jackhammer as it was in operation, violently shaking in a poorly functional simulation of a large drill.

After his terrible labouring ordeal was over, I suppose Trout thought that his employer would give him some less arduous work, but when that job finished he was retrenched, so to speak. To make matters worse, he had been let go without getting his full entitlement. Normally, you would think that was that and the remainder would never be seen. But Trout eventually managed to get fully paid and, by the standards of labouring jobs in London at the time, he was paid reasonably well.

Trout was looking for easier work and he had some money in his pocket. Just as he was in this condition and frame of mind one of our many acquaintances at the Kings Head, an ex-pat like ourselves, returned from Amsterdam where he had brought several sheets of blotters.

'Blotters' were a drug delivery system technology of the day so they need a little explanation. One way of making LSD trips was to make a solution of the drug and then dip sheets of thick paper into the liquid to soak some up. Then the sheets were dried. Each piece of paper treated in this way ended up having acid dispersed through it. The sheets usually had a repetitive pattern on them to make it easier to cut them up into individual trips. Often the design was a pattern of squares where each square contained the same small picture or other graphic. This was a way of identifying the batch, and of facilitating the division into individual trips as each square was cut from the sheet and taken as a separate trip.

I'm not sure how many trips were in the sheet that Trout bought but it could easily have been up to 300, as it would have been if it were divided into 15 squares by 20. The number was certainly something approaching this, and Trout anticipated multiplying his investment several times.

They say that you should start as you intend to continue, so that first night Trout had the trips did not augur well for his proposed business enterprise. Trout and I each took a trip and about half a dozen of our fellow drinkers at the Kings Head also bought trips. One really crazy South African guy bought one and took it, and then did the same again two more times. I don't know how that ended up going but I dread to think. Even at the time I was surprised and thought it a bad idea.

The acid was more or less evenly distributed through the sheet of blotters but it seems that the ones in the very bottom row were the most powerful. This would make perfect sense if the sheets had been hung up to dry. The trips we had all taken that first night were from one edge of the sheet and that must have been at the bottom when the sheet was dried.

Amidst the wheeling and dealing and strange goings-on of that evening in the pub, Trout and I told Charlie about our impending eviction from Bramham Gardens and he said we could come and stay at his place at West Harrow. Charlie was a short solid Cockney with curly fair locks. No one knew exactly what Charlie's main means of support was but he was known to be an operator; that is, doing a bit of this and that and the other. Charlie's reputation was strangely spivvy, especially given that many of the people we knew were multiple substance abusers, with all that went with that, so he must have been up to something special or unusual.

Why Charlie came from the East End, lived at West Harrow, and socialised in Earls Court I do not know. Or, to put it the other way round, why he operated in and socialised around Earls Court and some other inner London precincts but lived at West Harrow was part of the mystery that was Charlie.

Charlie also had one of the trips and when the pub shut we headed off with him. One of the barmen from the Kings Head, Jeremy, who was only about 18 years old, had also taken a trip and decided to join us for the rest of the evening.

The train trip from Earls Court necessarily involved at least one change of trains, usually at Rayners Lane station. But there were a variety of ways that could have been used to get to West Harrow and that first night we changed trains more than once. This meant that we were at a few different stations on the way and I'm not sure at which one this particularly memorable event took place, but it may have been Acton Town. We are drunk and tripping, loudly joking, laughing, and generally carrying on in a ridiculous manner, when Trout jumps down off the railway platform and onto the tracks. Then he goes to lie down across the tracks as you might imagine someone tied up in an old western. The moment his back touched the live rail there was a tremendous flash and Trout was thrown off the tracks seemingly completely unharmed.

Why he wasn't killed or injured I don't know. I guess the way he did it, lying backwards, meant that when the great charge of electricity surged through him, all his muscles contracted and fired him forward, away from the danger.

Even in our hotwired states we were taken aback and momentarily shocked. Trout climbed back onto the platform laughing with his naughty schoolboy giggle and looking surprised, presumably at both his own actions and their result. When I asked him why he had tried to lie across the tracks he offered an explanation along the lines that he imagined himself back in Brisbane, where the electricity wires were suspended overhead. Then the loud joking and laughing recommenced.

It carried on all the way to Charlie's place. The night had become a bizarre adventure. Three of us had never been to Charlie's place or even that part of London. Everything was new, and even the suburb of white, paired, semi-detached houses and their little gardens was interesting in the night light.

When we got to Charlie's place we sorted out our sleeping facilities. That is, we were shown and chose two rooms, before we settled down to drinking and smoking and talking and laughing. As time went by, almost imperceptibly, the mood changed from a tremendous high to something very dark and horrible. Charlie's stinking feet ended up being the butt of all the jokes for what seemed to be the last half hour, and then we went to bed.

As I lay there tired but still buzzing, I could hear Charlie downstairs washing his feet. The pain and insecurity really touched me. I had been so out of it that I hadn't known whether Charlie's feet really stank or they had baselessly become a running joke, but clearly Charlie had been sitting through all that feeling who knows how dreadful. In my mind, somewhere was the idea that any one of us could have ended up the victim of such a personal humiliation.

On the bed in my new room, I was now wanting to crash but I continued to lay there for some time trying to get my thoughts together and find the proper forgetfulness, the wonderful lethargy that is sleep. At one point while I waited for it to come I got up and looked out of the window. I didn't know if it was day or night, and eventually all I had was the reasoning that said 'I can see the street lights are on so it must be night'.

Inertia and Grace

Trout's purchase of the sheet of blotters was meant to be a business matter but things turned out differently. Ensconced in Charlie's Place at West Harrow, we would start each day hung-over and whatever the state is that follows the excesses of taking a trip. It wouldn't be a case of 'Never again!' but we would begin thinking that we would not take a trip that day. Inevitably, however, at some point, usually by mid or late afternoon, boredom would set in and we would have another blotter. While this was the usual order, I do remember one morning when we had only been up for about an hour before we found ourselves dropping another one, but that was exceptional.

I thought our move out to West Harrow was a complete non-event for the neighbours because I don't think I had spotted a single one, but someone had been watching us. About the second or third afternoon that we were at Charlie's place there was a knock on the door. It was a woman from across the road. We were all in our early twenties so Vera seemed quite old to us; she must have been in her late thirties going on forty. Vera introduced herself as a neighbour just popping over to say hello and to welcome us to the street. I'm often oblivious to these things and so it was on this occasion. Vera's husband was at work or out somewhere but she clearly didn't have that long. The four of us had a cup of tea and chatted, but the tea had barely gone done when Trout and Vera adjourned, almost raced, upstairs. Ten minutes later, if that, Vera was shooting out the front door wishing us a good day.

While we were living out at West Harrow on our trip bender, another Trout admirer entered the frame. Grace was part of a circle of wild southern African ex-pats. She was a kind of nominal South African or Zimbabwean (these were white colonials and the war was just over so most of them still thought of themselves as Rhodesians). In fact, Grace came from Zambia.

At this time, Grace took Trout under her wing. Most afternoons at West Harrow, Grace would turn up bearing a gift. On at least one occasion it was a bottle of scotch and in the end she gave Trout some credit cards.

Grace's little gang was well versed in the use of stolen credit cards. This was before the era of ATMs, and the proper electronic banking we have today. The misuse of credit cards in west London at the time really revolved around the presentation of the self as an ex-pat so that the shop assistant, or whoever, presumed the user was a tourist, with money. Trout may have managed to use one or other of the credit cards but he really didn't have the level of sophisticated duplicity needed to carry out the scam.

Despite her criminality, Grace was a lovely girl. Her affection for Trout and her need for male companionship and support were obvious. She was trying to be kind, and to move forward, but her attentions were misplaced. Not that Trout was not a generous soul, he was, but Grace was looking for a stable friend, to cling to, and Trout was on a wild ride. After Trout and I left West Harrow, we still ran into Grace from time to time. There were still connections but the circles had turned and were no longer locked together. Many of Grace's associates lived in north London while we made our way nearly back to the greater SW5-SW10 precinct.

The more or less daily taking of trips was almost invariably followed by a train journey to west London and an evening of drinking. Most often the destination was Earls Court and the Kings Head was still very much our regular haunt.

While drinking somehow went naturally with tripping, the same could not be said for eating. Acid was not conducive to it, so eating hardly ever happened. I recall one day buying a meat pie and trying to consume it. The first bite felt like some horrible globulous thing swelling in my mouth, so I spat it out and threw the rest of the pie in the bin.

As time went by under this relentless regime of LSD and alcohol consumption, our health was really suffering. As well as eating being almost non-existent, what sleep I did have was often very disturbed. I rapidly became very run down, and it must have been showing.

Towards the end of my time at West Harrow, I arranged to meet several expats at a pub in Earls Court for lunch. To get to Earls Court, I would catch the tube from West Harrow to Rayners Lane and then change onto the Piccadilly Line to Earls Court. This particular day, having changed trains at Rayners Lane, I got most of the way to Earls Court before falling asleep. I woke with a start at some unrecognised station and jumped off the train. I realised what had happened and went across the railway platform and caught the next train back.

This is one of those things where it is hard to reconcile my memory with the existing documentary evidence. As I recall it, this station was Aldgate East on the District Line but it must have been something like Manor House on the Piccadilly Line. I say this because when the next train came and I got on board I worked out that I was fourteen stops beyond my destination which was ironic as I had begun 14 stops the other side of Earls Court. When that very familiar object that is the tube map is examined, however, there must be some problem in my recollection because it doesn't seem to fit.

I did not bother getting off the train as it went back through Earls Court because the pubs would have been closed for their afternoon break. By the time I was back at West Harrow I was feeling exhausted and needed a rest from all the travelling. Later, however, Trout and I ended up taking another trip and heading out to the pub, as per usual.

Afterthought

Years later I met Trout again one afternoon in Queensland when I bought him a few drinks, him still being on the bones of his arse, by which I mean he was completely broke. Different things have different priorities for different people. One person will remember one event and the other another. And so it was as we discussed our time together in London, but, understandably, Trout returned several times to the topic of Grace. I don't know if he regretted her loss or not. I know that if it were me, I would have, because Grace was a lovely girl and she loved Trout, and he needed someone like her to help him through life.

Re-entering West Harrow

The chaos at West Harrow couldn't last and after about a month Charlie evicted Trout and I. Trout found a lounge at a squat somewhere but I found myself without a roof. In sheer desperation, the evening after I had been thrown out, I went back to Charlie's Place.

I didn't have key and the house provided a difficult challenge. I was adept at slipping a standard latch with a bit of plastic — credit cards were good — but Charlie's locks were better than the average. I walked around the house and climbed up to the first floor bedroom windows but I couldn't get in. I wasn't that surprised because I knew that security was a high priority for Charlie.

The situation was like a puzzle; there had to be a way in and I was determined to find it. In the end the old plastic strip came good. A window in the laundry had one of those little levers that enable the user to have the window securely closed or to use the notches to leave it open at various set points. This window was latched and the little arm with the notches had a metal band on it that stopped the window being opened beyond the first or second notch. Once I had unlatched it with the piece of plastic (I may have used a bit of a plastic bottle that I ripped into sturdy strips), I was able to get two fingers in and use the strip to gradually loosen the screws that attached the latch arm to the window itself. The screws were old, more than a little rusted and not very tight, otherwise I would never have been able to work them loose with the plastic. Once one screw was loose I could more quickly finish undoing it with my fingers. Then the other screw was removed in the same fashion.

This whole exercise must have taken some time and I would not have had the courage to do it except that I was breaking into the house in which I had been living. If I had been challenged, I suppose that I would have claimed to have locked myself out or lost the key.

Once I was inside I reattached the latch. I liked the neatness of it but I also avoided breaking and entering if I could. Then I went back upstairs to my old room and tried to go to sleep. I was pumped with adrenalin and anxious about Charlie's return but I think I managed to get to sleep.

When Charlie turned up some hours later the confrontation did not turn out as I expected. I thought that there would be a fierce fight but, while it was made perfectly clear that I would have to leave the next day, Charlie was mostly keen to know how I got in. He had thought that his house was safe and wanted to make sure that it would be in the future. I explained how I had got in and went back to sleep. I sleep surprisingly soundly but once I was up I had to go and so off I went.

Philbeach Gardens and the Royal Borough of Kensington and Chelsea

People capture territory. Having sat in a particular seat on a bus or in a cinema, a person often feels safer there and will seek out the same seat or one nearby the next time. So, having been evicted from West Harrow where did I go but back to the familiar, if not necessarily safe, surrounds of SW5 and SW10.

A tremendous amount of bravado is born of naivety, especially with me, and I simply started looking around the areas that I knew, searching for an empty house with the goal of turning it into a squat.

I found a beautiful five-storey building at 70 Philbeach Gardens. The windows facing the street were boarded up and the front door had a great big bold lock attached but anyone familiar with the art of screw driving could let him or herself in, as I did.

There was a wonderful bar on the second or third floor that looked out onto the park behind with its grass, bench seats and picturesque wintry trees. It was such a truly lovely place and I immediately settled in.

My comings and goings for the next few days seemed to pass unnoticed and in that time I got a job sweeping the streets of the Royal Borough of Kensington and Chelsea. The council officer that employed me was prepared to give a young Australian a go but the other street sweepers were not so generous.

This was my first real encounter with the English working poor. There were about a dozen street sweepers working out of the little depot and most of them could not afford to live in the Borough. Several lived in remote south eastern suburbs of London. The weekly wage was less than £70 and £16 of that might go on the tube fare. I wondered how they could keep their families on these wages.

I had recently become familiar with poverty but I had not really seen at such close quarters those whose long-term prospects would be to just keep their heads above water. The Royal Borough employees I worked with counted how many cigarettes they lent each other and would not allow a debt of more than three to be accumulated.

The council employees also expected the new bloke to take them to the pub and buy them a round. This was not possible for me. As it was my breakfast was a bottle of milk taken off someone's doorstep on my way to the depot. This had been my regular morning meal for some time. I preferred the gold top bottles. The other street sweepers were, however, unaware of my mean circumstances and once I did not buy them the round of drinks I was on the outer.

Another of my main problems as a novice street sweeper, or footpath sweeper really, was being inappropriately conscientious. I swept too thoroughly and that meant too slowly. The very first day I swept away studiously all morning but early in the afternoon I was sweeping beside Cadogan Square when the gardener came over to the fence and struck up a conversation. I only spoke to him for a couple of minutes but as I did I saw a Borough vehicle cross the street I was sweeping two corners ahead at Cadogan Gardens. Then the vehicle crossed over the street on the next corner, from where the occupants looked down and saw me talking to the gardener. I knew straight away that they would think that I was lazy and had spent most of the day talking.

With the other workers unhappy that I didn't shout them a drink and the supervisor under the false impression that I was a shirker, I stood little chance. At the end of the first week I was given one week's notice. On that Friday, a little after I was informed of my impending departure, the union representative came up and promised to help. But then he soon reappeared and said they wouldn't be changing their minds so I might as well take it easy.

The hopelessness of the situation was confirmed at the beginning of the next week. I was clearly at the bottom of the pecking order and had been given what was probably the most arduous beat to sweep that first week. The following week, however, one of the most senior sweepers was ill and his job should have gone to someone higher up the seniority list but it was given to me because, I think, they didn't expect me to do anything and the longer beats required more sweeping.

The truly prime area that I had been allocated included Harrods and the few streets adjacent to it. All of the paths in my care were inside the near-triangle formed by Brompton Road, Sloane Street, Beauchamp Place and Pont Street. This was a salubrious area, and in the heart of it was a large home with a good size garden. Who knows what that property was worth? I don't know who lived there but each day when I swept up to its front gate a security guy would come along and talk to me. As he chatted away he would throw solid rubber balls for his two Staffordshire terriers to fetch. I loved those dark, chocolaty balls of muscle but I was also confident that if they bit someone they would not let go.

As well as seeing the more than comfortable streets and houses of Knightsbridge, I discovered that the regular council employee had a mildly lucrative sideline sweeping the driveways of residences in the area. Some of these were private houses but more than one was an embassy or consulate.

That second week of my two-week career, I was also given some overtime by the Borough. Someone had complained about the noise of the rubbish truck and crew, so a special evening of street sweeping and rubbish removal was organised. We were encouraged to yell out basic instructions to each other and to bang the bins about while the lorries put on their own aural display as part of our extraordinary detritus elimination exercise.

During the first week of my job for the Royal Borough, Trout and Gerry Tunk joined me in the Philbeach Gardens mansion. Gerry Tunk was a Zimbabwean with a slightly colourful recent past, whose escape from the country when it was Rhodesia would have made a nice scene for Steve McQueen.

Trout and Gerry Tunk were both delighted by the wonderful house and its great view. Pretending to have cocktails at the bar while taking in the scene, we imagined ourselves millionaires. It was too good to last and it didn't. The population explosion probably hastened the end. A couple of days after the other two joined me in the opulent squat, I came back from sweeping the streets of Knightsbridge to find my few belongings sitting on the street and the building more rigorously re-secured.

That evening I saw Trout at the Kings Head. He had been the only one at home when the owner or developer turned up with two large heavies who smashed their way in. Trout had been terrified and panicked as they pursued him through the building. They might have just wanted to persuade him to pick up his stuff and not come back but he wasn't taking any chances. He ended up bolting up on top of the building and then across a neighbour's roof before making his way back down to the street. When he went back later on all of our stuff was on the street and he had picked up his gear. While Trout was still loitering nearby Gerry had turned up, been told of the situation and picked up his belongings before heading off to find somewhere else to crash.

Halford Road

After my fraught night at Charlie's place and the brief grand illusion of Philbeach Gardens, I put my mind to finding somewhere safer. Gerry Tunk had gone off to stay with South African friends and Trout had persuaded his former flatmates at Putney that he really needed to crash there for a few days. I gathered that they had put him up before and weren't that keen, but given his acute accommodation crisis they had agreed to take him in on the condition that it was temporary. That left me as an individual vagrant and I needed to find somewhere to stay urgently.

I knew quite a few people in squats and I was hopeful of finding accommodation in one but I somehow always heard about the vacancies just a little too late. I usually found out when someone told me about another person moving in where a fourth party had left. For some reason, I've always felt that in many things I've had to do the whole thing myself where others would have received some kind of entré or assistance. On some occasions this appears to be a product of my lack of confidence or shyness, so I don't put myself forward in a friendly way at the opportune moment, but at other times it seems that others assume that I don't need any help because I can be resourceful. Whatever the reason, it now appeared that finding a secure squat was also going to be like that, and it was.

I wasn't looking for a hovel but, obviously, my first such attempt at Philbeach Gardens had been too ambitious so I started to look for something more appropriate to my station. I was especially keen to find a place that wasn't overseen by a ruthless developer with large thuggy mates.

As memory does not serve me perfectly on this point, I'm not sure if I found a place and then some Scottish drunks moved in above me, or if someone told me about the place below where the Scottish drunks were and I moved in there. It might just have been that someone suggested this row of terraces in Fulham because several of them were vacant and a couple of the houses were already squatted.

Whatever way I got there, I found a vacant ground floor of a terrace house and started to investigate. The front window was covered with corrugated iron, presumably both to stop it being smashed and to make it harder to break into the unit. Apart from that, the security was pretty basic. I unscrewed a bolt and then used a bit of plastic or whatever to click open the standard lock.

Nothing was broken in this entry, and I would have tried to avoid that and to fix anything that was broken because I understood that such damage and its non-repair was the difference between squatting and breaking and entering. Likewise, I believed that the breaking of a lock was a crime but the replacement of a lock with one to which you had the key was not; so that's what I would have done if I had to.

Once inside I searched around in the near pitch black and found that the place consisted of a corridor on the left with two bedrooms on the right and then a little kitchen. Attached to the rear of the house was also a functional toilet.

The water was on so that left electricity as the remaining necessary utility. I had been told that in many cases with these vacant houses and apartments all you had to do was to replace the main fuse. Once I located it, I grabbed the white insulating material at the back of the biggest fuse. Quickly, and nervously, I reefed it out. Nothing happened, which was great. The fuse was missing. I rolled up a bit of alfoil from the inside of a cigarette pack and slipped it between the two metal prongs. This was the moment, and then there was nothing to do but to stick it in and hope for the best. Even more quickly than I had pulled the fuse out, I jammed it back in. I wasn't electrocuted, and one of the lights inside the flat went on. The squat was go.

Now that I had light I could check the place out in more detail. There was a bed in each of the rooms and the kitchen had a little oven with a single hot plate on top. This was good. I felt I had myself a new home.

Relaxed and seemingly secure, I set off for a few beers at the Kings Head. When I was there I ran into Charlie and told him about my new digs. He asked what the address was. A bit like how you might have a new mobile phone and not know its number because you don't ring yourself, I had to explain to Charlie where it was because I didn't know the name of the street let alone the number. The important thing was that it was there, I knew how to get there and I had access. I think the address was 118 Halford Road, Fulham, that is, about the third last terrace on the left hand side as you walk away from North End Road, opposite the Fulham Primary School.

The following night I ran into Moira. Moira was one of a group of young Irish women that I had met at the Richmond Hotel in Earls Court Road. These girls were planning to move to Australia, and several of them did. For some reason, Moira had taken a shine to me and the feeling was mutual.

On this occasion I probably found Moira and her mates at the Richmond, that's where we usually met, although it also might have been at the Houghton Club the other side of West Cromwell Road. The Houghton Club had that thin 'classy' veneer you would see in a lot of these small clubs and it reminded me of Arthur Daley's establishment, but it was mainly frequented by west London Irish.

I was surprised that Moira relented and came back, as much because she was a good or goodish Irish Catholic girl, and as

109

much because she had declined the offer to come back with me to Bramham Gardens. When I asked her about the change of mind she said that she had got the feeling that I did not really want her to go back to Bramham Gardens. She was probably right. The mode of entry would have put off all but the most desperate of young ladies and then once inside she would have been confronted by what one of our very few visitors described as 'wall-to-wall rubbish'.

With a tantalising combination of embarrassment, nervous pride and anticipation, Moira and I made our way back to Halford Road and onto the bed in the front bedroom. I had slept there the previous night, my first night in my new home, but obviously the sleeping had not been very energetic because Moira and I barely got into the action when the bed collapsed. Shocked, we both burst out laughing. A quick investigation revealed that bed was assembled but the bolts that held the base to the two ends were only sitting in place and the nuts had not been attached.

Not long after this, maybe two or three weeks later, Moira and I broke up. I don't know why we did because I was still very fond of her. I think she was just going in another direction and saw that I wasn't going anywhere good. Not long after we split, I remember running into Moira again at the Richmond only to find that she now had a new beau. I was happy; I wanted her to be happy.

It was just after Moira's and my parting that Trout arrived back in London. He had been down surfing at Biarritz on the very southern end of the French Atlantic coast and had managed to get a little work there but whatever income he had made was gone. There was a room to spare in my new Halford Road home and Trout moved straight in. Trout was very taken with our new circumstances and commented enthusiastically on the move up from the situation at Bramham Gardens.

A couple of weeks later, I was in the Kings Head one night and I ran into Larry. Apparently, Larry had been living a life of dashing depravity in Germany, working on building sites in Wiesbaden, but breaking a few rules as well and living it up on the profits. Larry has just got back and he happened to be digs-free so he also moved in. The bedrooms were a reasonable size and from what I recall Larry moved into my room.

It didn't make that much difference anyway as a couple of months after Larry's return another refugee from our hometown, Gaffney, came to London and moved into the other room. So, if I remember rightly, there was Trout and Gaffney in the second room with Larry and I in the front one. Other combinations were possible because all I really remember on the issue was that I had moved into the front room when I first opened up the squat and there I stayed. And Trout was the second to arrive and he moved into the other room when he got there.

My third relationship with
the Corner House

Once I was established in Halford Road I found that, in addition to the chronic lack of money, jobs and so on, I had an important basic problem. The squat had a heater and a little oven with a single plate cooktop but it did not have a bathroom. The lack of a bathroom was not unusual for this kind of area in England. This, however, was a time of transition, which was a time of hardness, especially for older people.

In the years and decades leading up to the 1980s it was common for whole streets of these little houses not to have bathrooms. The inhabitants would use the facilities in the local community baths once a week, or so. As time moved on, however, standards changed and tenants were replaced by owner-occupiers when more affluent people moved into the area. The new residents installed bathrooms into their houses. This meant that less and less people used the community baths, and the people who were left that did use the public facilities were the poor or the elderly, and usually both. The public baths became social services and this was the Thatcher era, so public facilities were being closed in one community after another. I imagined old ladies who had lived in an area since they were young suddenly finding themselves without any bathing facilities. Those poor old people I thought.

As 118 Halford Road was an unimproved property it didn't have a bathroom. Crucially, however, there was also no local public convenience. After a few increasingly grubby days, I came up with a very cheeky and unlikely solution. Halford Road was only about twenty minutes' walk from the Corner House where Trout and I had camped on the roof with its bathroom on the second floor. So I went around there with my half-p entrance and had a shower. When Trout moved in he did the same, as I think both Larry and Gaffney did while they were at Halford Road.

Initially I went around to shower thinking that if I were challenged I would just say that I was staying with the South Africans (who were very likely to be long gone). But, in the event, I was never challenged, and doing it during the day when people were likely to be at work, I think I only ever once walked over there with my soap and towel to find the shower being used.

Unfortunately, another convenience problem emerged a couple of weeks after I began using the bathroom at the Corner House. When I first gained access to the Halford Road flat it had a perfectly functional toilet out the back. All too soon, however, this was ruined by our short-sighted neighbours upstairs, or one of their associates.

A few weeks after I moved into the ground floor at Halford Road, someone stole some piping from the upstairs flat. Whether it was one of the residents, or one of their mates, or just someone who had access to the flat, I never knew, but I was told that copper pipes had been stolen. I'm not sure what the theft did to the situation up there but it produced a solid drip downstairs that was right over the toilet.

In response to the drip I installed a very large umbrella in the ceiling of the lean-to directly over the toilet to protect its users. While the level of protection provided by the umbrella was reasonable, the setup was well short of ideal.

The free flow of electricity

It is strange to look back and think that the scrap of alfoil from the inside of a cigarette packet would maintain the electricity supply for the whole time that I would live in Halford Road; and how productive that little piece of aluminium would be.

One winter's day a little after Trout had joined me in the flat, the heater broke. It just suddenly stopped working so we unplugged the device and turned it upside down to check out its innards. The element was a single coil of metal and the whole rest of the appliance was simply there to protect people from the coil and to let air heat up and flow out of the top. We stretched the spring-like wire until the two ends hooked each other and turned the appliance back on again. There was a quick bright glow as the touching parts welded together and then the heater resumed normal service. We righted the heater and it continued to work for a few days but then it stopped again and we had to repeat the process.

After about the third time the heater had broken and been repaired in this manner we left it upside down to make it easier to fix. It was never righted again, it never broke again and it was never turned off again for the whole time we were there. For the remainder of our time at Halford Road the heater faithfully pumped out its rays of heat keeping our little kitchen toasty warm.

One day towards the end of December 1980, Larry, Trout and I were sitting in the kitchen wearing nothing but jeans and T-shirts, hot after a walk to the North End Road markets — in fact, Stan was sitting there without any top on — when this great cheer went up from across the road. The kids at Fulham Primary were at play in their morning break when it started to snow. Once again, this was one the nicest moments of my whole time in London.

Before we were thrown out of the squat, a bill arrived from the power company for a few hundred pounds. It was never seriously considered.

Sneakiness and criminality; or, the Bertie Beetle and the bottle of wine

I remember my first theft quite clearly. I was about three years old and I was standing in a department store beside my mother and my baby sister, who was in the pram. I had asked my mother for a Bertie Beetle but she had said no.

For those who don't know, the Bertie Beetle was a delicious — almost irresistible — chocolate filled with pieces of honeycomb. Each of these sweets was shaped like a flattish bug and wrapped in alfoil, which completed the look of a brightly coloured, poker-dotted, beetle.

This day, these delicious beetles of chocolate and honeycomb were too much. After my mother had declined my request for a Bertie Beetle, I stood there beside her full skirt, facing the lollies while she was ordering something from the girl behind the counter. The crime was not premeditated; the moment appeared and I recognised it. I noticed that the shop assistant had walked several metres to the right and my mum was looking in her direction. I was standing to my mother's left where neither would observe me, so I took my chance. By which I mean, I quickly snatched the Bertie Beetle and then kept it concealed in my little hand.

No doubt my mum had other things on her mind and she didn't notice. And nor did she observe that, over the next few minutes as we moved around the shop, I sneakily peeled off the exciting and attractive aluminium foil wrapper and ate the chocolate treat one sneaky little bite after another. This moment was a simultaneous coming of awareness and of criminality. For good or for ill I have carried it with me ever since.

This leads me to one afternoon in Earls Court eighteen or nineteen years later. Somehow I had acquired a bottle of wine. I was headed up to the pub to meet friends so it wasn't convenient for me to carry the bottle around. I might have been walking along Trebovir Road when I noticed that a storm water drain was constructed in a way that a bottle, or some other object, could be safely secreted inside because even if it were to rain, the water would rush over or around the concealed space without disturbing it. I furtively looked about and then quickly put the bottle into the spied cavity. Then I headed off for a drink with my bottle nestled in what I judged would be a safe spot, beside the road under the edge of the footpath out of view.

I'm not sure when I returned to my public hidey-hole. It might have that night as I wandered home from an evening of social drinks or it might have been the next afternoon. What I'm sure about is that when I got back to the same corner I remembered the hole and the bottle. Once again I had a quick peek about and then reached into the concealed cavity. There it was. Off I went, with my regained refreshment. I was a lot more satisfied with my sneakiness than I was with the repossession of the drink.

Peter Lowe

What can you say about Peter Lowe? The two words that first spring to my mind are 'extreme' and 'street'. Those two words have a certain resonance but they mainly point only to the surface. Peter Lowe was the sort of bloke who would break into your squat and steal something one morning but then turn up with a present that afternoon. The present would be contaminated in one way or another; it would be either drugs or something stolen.

Many times it was drugs. He always had drugs, in which his taste was pretty catholic, and sometimes he had lots. At one point he kept coming around with a variety of things, including amyl nitrate. I'm sure that stuff has its place in the order of things but, to me, its damage to fun ratio is too high. I certainly remember, though, on many occasions a group of us sitting together and passing the little bottle around. Peter Lowe, Trout, Larry and I used to pass it around as we were chatting and drinking, giggling a lot of the time. As the participants' heads glowed red in succession; it was like a circle of globes with one going on after another. At other times it was as if there was only one bloodshot glowing head but it kept revolving around the circle, jumping from person to person.

Another time — and these durations might have overlapped — Peter Lowe had a lot of amphetamines. Speed was one of my weaknesses but we all partook. The four of us got into the habit of loading up on the speed, having a few drinks, often Fullers ESB at the Seven Stars on North End Road, and then hitting the pubs in Earls Court.

Needless to say this was a formula for disaster and it couldn't last long. The main problem really revolved around the fact that when we got drunk we still had a lot of energy. So instead of stopping, crashing and going home, we would keep going on like loose tappets, getting louder and louder but less and less rational and more disorderly. The whole thing could have gone very badly but the results were simply comical. After a week or two of this we were all banned from a variety of pubs, including most of our favourite haunts. So when the four of us would hit Earls Court Road of an afternoon or evening we had to split into two groups of two. Larry and Peter Lowe would head off to the Kings Head, which was their sole remaining regular venue, while Trout and I went to the Richmond, which was ours.

Both Larry and Peter Lowe were self-confessed opportunists but the latter saw chances, and took them, where no one else would even think of them. When the boat show was going to be held at the Earls Court Exhibition Centre, the local employment agencies advertised for security men for the event. The screening process must have had its limitations because both Larry and Peter Lowe went along for the day of training and were issued with their uniforms. Larry did his week or so of work, usually manning the main vehicle entrance. Peter Lowe didn't do the job but he kept his uniform. He would put it on and go up to the Exhibition Centre and have a free meal. I think that he did it every day for the duration of the show.

Peter Lowe had had a very interesting and unusual colonial upbringing. He possessed several passports, which had its advantages. Coupled with this, was the fact that despite his visage presenting to me as a scrawny junkie who had been roughed up and then slept rough after a rough night at the pub having previously outfitted himself at an army disposals shop, Peter Lowe had some kind of charisma, or was a very good liar, or both. He had some of the most beautiful and exotic girlfriends you could ever hope to meet and he would turn up with one in London having acquired her in South America or Africa or wherever. The rumour circulated, and many believed, that he used these beautiful women to carry the drugs. It was also said that he would travel from one location to another on different passports before re-entering the UK on a passport suggesting that his travels had been to only his most recent, innocent and unlikely location.

I've got to admit to being a little jealous of Peter Lowe and his womanising ways but he was just about as disaffected, cynical and angry and as one could get. He gave only the barest snippets away about his past, but you would have to think that there was something ugly there. He hated the police with a vengeance and repeated the story that an uncle of his was bashed and disfigured by the police, but the authorities held onto the line that the victim had done it to himself with the plastic fork with which he had been provided to eat his gaol meal.

Peter Lowe had a clear contempt for pretty well all and sundry, including himself. He said more than once that when he died he wanted his corpse to be chained to a post on the footpath and left to rot.

While his morals seemed lacking and his ethics were more than questionable, you had to give it to Peter Lowe in the guts department. He would go to a pub and, when the moment appeared, reach in through the bar and overhead to the cavity above where spirit bottles were stored, and grab one. The bottle would be under his jacket and he would leave in what would appear to be no particular hurry. He must have been watching for these opportunities more or less constantly.

Magic mushrooms

Sometimes the best-intentioned plans can go completely astray.

One day Larry, Trout and I went shopping on North End Road. We only had a few pounds and decided to be completely sensible and to buy a couple of weeks' supply of root vegetables. Then we headed off home to Halford Road carrying several pounds of potatoes, carrots and onions. Who knows, we might even have had some sweet potatoes.

We hadn't been back long and were, as usual, sitting around our toasty kitchen drinking cups of tea and smoking cigarettes when there was a knock and Peter Lowe comes in with a fine young Englishman with wavy brown hair and slightly crusty attire. Peter Lowe introduces his companion as Mark. Mark, it turns out, is just back from Glastonbury where he has been doing a bit of nature frolicking and plundering. He has a small brown paper bag of magic mushrooms that he gives to us and which we gratefully accept. I'd seen gold tops in Australia and these were similar but much smaller.

It soon became apparent that the magic offering was designed to get us to let Mark stay in our squat. Mark seemed a nice enough guy, but we didn't know him. We were a tight crew and weren't looking for a new shipmate. We suggested that he try upstairs where the Scottish drinkers resided. He understandably wasn't interested in that, and the two of them headed off, leaving the little brown bag of mischief.

We didn't immediately have the mushrooms but they were not going to be left forever; so a little later that afternoon the conversation turned to the ingestion of mushies. We all had some limited experience but not of this particular variety and weren't sure what was the best way to go about it. Sautéing them in butter was one option that was considered, and another was the time-honoured omelette. Eventually, being cautious and sensible, we decided that a safe but reasonably effective way to ingest their psychotropic contents would be to make tea with the mushrooms. I think this was Trout's suggestion.

So we made the brew as you would a regular tea but with both the tea leaves and the mushrooms in the teapot. It didn't taste too bad and we drank the contents, which was only about a small cup each.

It wasn't long before things started to go haywire. We began lobbing things at each other and laughing. Trout's giggling was the most prominent but quickly we were all into it. The gentle lobbing of things at each other became a full on food fight using the vegetables that we had bought earlier that day. Larry, Trout and I were now launching around the flat throwing vegetables at each other and laughing; laughing at the near misses and laughing at the hits.

From what I recall, there were only four lights in the little ground floor flat; one in each bedroom, one in the hall and one in the kitchen. As we were furiously running around, throwing vegetables and laughing, someone turned off all the lights. The lights were then incorporated into the game in this way: all of the lights would be off for most of the time but every few seconds someone would flash one of them on for a fraction of a second. This we thought was hilarious. For that brief burst, which might be from any one of the four globes, you would just get a flash of this dynamic and anarchic scene. Anyone of us could be anywhere and the light would catch as we launched and laughed, and you would also just catch sight of a carrot or a potato in mid-air. Of course, we would all use the flash of information to throw vegetables at each other, guessing where our prey would be, as we moved about, while trying to avoid the missiles thrown by the other two.

Very soon the vegetables became parts of vegetables but that just multiplied the potential weapons and our intermittently strobed running, throwing, hitting, missing, avoiding and laughing carried on at a furious rate. In this wild confusion, the beds and what little other furniture we had were being knocked over and strewn about.

While this game seemed completely chaotic, and had begun in the kitchen, it was mainly played in the hallway and the two bedrooms with no one going any further than just inside the kitchen. The table, chairs, stove and permanent heater were in there, and that could have been disastrous.

The furious activity was exhilarating but it used a lot of energy and eventually we stopped, puffing, but still laughing. The lights were now back on and we could see that the flat looked like it had been hit by a vegetable tornado, which in a way it had.

Once the scene wore in we decided we had to get out. As we walked down the hall to the front door we surveyed the carnage in the bedrooms. Going past the front room, Trout noticed that there was still a bedside cupboard standing so he walked in and pushed it over. Then we headed out the door and started making our way towards Earls Court. The constant laughing and lurching about continued into our journey. We were almost completely out of control. It was if we were three again — three giant three year olds — and our immediate surrounds was a playground.

On the way we found a cushion shaped like a cat. We picked it up and started running with it, passing it to one another like it was a rugby ball. We ran and laughed and threw but we also did crazy things. We ran up, along and over fences, and we ran straight over cars. This was completely inexcusable but for us these objects had lost a lot of the social rules governing their treatment; they had been reduced to toys.

We ran in, over and around the obstacles, passing the cat cushion rugby style, in the light rain, all the way to Earls Court. When we were in the final street before Earls Court Road, the cushion was accidentally thrown under a car where we just left it because it had suddenly lost its interest and value. By the time we got to the pub, the intoxication caused by the magic mushrooms had been largely worked off by our furious activity and what remained was quickly pacified by the beer. We were still tripping a little, but now it was down to a buzz rather than an overwhelming energy.

After a few beers at the Kings Head, we had calmed down and we decided to head back to the squat. Not far into our return journey, we came across the cat-cushion again. We picked it up and carried it back. A little running and rugby passing was involved but the energy had gone now and this was more of a reminder of the trip there. Running over cars was no longer an option.

When we arrived back at the flat we were reasonably sober and straight, and we were completely appalled by the mess of strewn furniture and bedding surrounded by a carpet of vegetable pieces. After sitting for a little while in the kitchen, our disgust was transformed into a righteous indignation and a power. Nearly as furiously as we had played our running and throwing game, we went about the flat collecting the vegetables pieces and righting the furniture. Pretty soon the whole place was back in order. If anything, it was even neater than it had been prior to our drugged antics.

All this had taken place over the course of a few hours and it was still only just into the evening. Sitting around the kitchen in our newly spruced flat we quickly found ourselves at a loose end so we boiled up the kettle again and poured the water into the teapot. This second cup of tea was surprisingly like the first. The effect of the second cup of tea was also quite like that of the first but it would be an exaggeration to say that we did it all again.

Not long after we had the tea it was obvious that the potion's action was going to be similar but it was less and we had the experience of the previous mushroom tea. So, almost as soon as we started giggling again with a nervous infantile energy, we decided to head out the door and back up to the pub. We sort of re-enacted the first journey, still running and laughing and carrying on. A casual observer would have thought us out of control but we were not the euphoric menaces that we had been on the previous trip.

Once up at the Kings Head, again, we were much more quickly under control and the night became a pleasant chat with new acquaintances. Our new friends were having a small party at their place, which was not far away in Child's Street or Redfield Lane. The party didn't last long and then we were making our way back to Halford Road, sated and calm.

If this whole episode had been done on speed or coke, we would have been complete wrecks the next day but the intoxication had been worn off by our extremely energetic carryings on. We all got up in good spirits and spent a lot of the morning laughing at our ridiculous antics of the previous day.

Curried rabbit stew

Rabbits were a pest in Australia. In the Burra district, as in many parts of outback Australia, there were times you could drive around and look at the country and not see a speck of green between the ground and a height of about one metre. It was as if some gigantic organic vacuum cleaner had gone around clearing this bottom layer of all vegetation. The vacuum cleaner was the rabbit and rabbits had eaten everything from the ground up to the highest point they could reach stretched upright by standing on their hind legs.

When I was a child, people around Burra used traps to catch the rabbits and any excess they caught was given away or sold. All other regular foods were sold in shops, but rabbits were sold in pubs. And, being scrawny little things, they were always sold in pairs. I guess a pair made about the same amount as a chicken. Someone who had caught rabbits to spare would turn up at the pub and sell pairs for a dollar each.

My dad must have liked rabbits, or the bloke up the pub who used to sell them. My mum wasn't keen on bunnies as she wasn't keen on any game, including ducks and fish. I think she preferred things from the shop.

As the oldest child with no other little boys in the immediate neighbourhood, I spent a lot of my preschool days following my mum around. After I left home, I began cooking for myself based on what I could remember my mum doing. Skinned rabbits, I recalled, she soaked in water in the sink before cooking them. I think she used to bake them, but years later in Adelaide I developed my secret recipe for curried rabbit stew.

The recipe wasn't difficult and not really secret; I don't believe anyone ever asked for it. The method was developed in this way. I had a basic recipe for lamb stew, including a fair proportion of vegetables, that I used a few times. I found that adding just a level teaspoon of curry powder to the stew right at the start added a little something without making the stew into a curry. Then, one time I got a rabbit at the Adelaide markets. Following my mum's habit, I soaked it in the sink and cooked it *a la* my lamb stew recipe but added a bit more curry powder so that it actually was a curried rabbit stew. I cooked it very slowly to make it juicy and tender and it worked a treat.

One day Larry, Trout and I were browsing along the North End Road markets when I noticed some rabbits for sale. The rabbits must have been cheap otherwise I can't imagine why we would have bought one. No doubt I was telling Larry and Trout about the delights of my curried rabbit stew and I assume they went along happy to eat anything so long as I cooked it.

I might digress here just for a moment on Trout's accomplishments as a chef. Trout's attitude was that you had to eat because it was necessary for survival. Neil, who I used to live with in West Kens', used to say, 'If you don't eat you don't shit, and if you don't shit you die'. Culinary-wise, I think Trout was from the same school. He would knock very basic things together so that they were palatable, or approached palatability. The worse example I recall was when he started out making scrambled eggs and just that second or so too late changed his mind and prepared an omelette. The result was granules of oily fried egg floating in a milky soup. Not recommended.

Trout did, however, have his own secret recipe and, strangely enough, it was more than just edible. Almost everyone knows that the Americans eat 'peanut butter and jelly' sandwiches and that banana can be added to the composition. In Australia we would normally use jam rather than jelly because jam is more common. Anything sweet, however, can be substituted for the jelly, and Trout would make peanut butter, honey, banana and lettuce sandwiches. The odd bit was the lettuce but it worked a treat so long as you used iceberg because you really couldn't taste it but the lettuce enhanced the sandwich by adding a juicy crunch.

I don't recall Larry being much of a cook at the time but he has certainly developed a few tricks since and over the years I have had some tasty feeds that he has prepared.

As I was saying, I assume that both Larry and Trout agreed to my planned rabbit meal mainly because they were glad to have someone prepare something. Following the method described above, I filled a large pot and had it cooking on the lowest setting available. That setting would still have been too high for most things but the pot was a good size with a thick base and it was filled nearly to the brim with rabbit, vegetables and a lot of liquid.

This was going to take some time so we adjourned to a pub. As we were not going out for the evening but just having a few beers we headed down to a pub in Fulham. The reader probably knows where this is heading and you may be right, but perhaps not in all of the details.

There is nothing like just going down to the hotel for one or two for you to really enjoy your beers. Naturally, we had one and then another and then another and got into the swing of things. Half the people in the pub were going back to someone's house for an impromptu party and we were invited. The house wasn't far the other side of North End Road, possibly just past Fulham Broadway, and so we headed there as soon as the pub closed.

It was a great little party. There was an interesting mix of people including a few locals, people from other parts of Britain, and some other colonials.

At the party, one of my better mysteries was solved. Some weeks previously I had been at the Kings Head at closing time. As we were being urged out I was one of the last patrons left in the hotel. By the time I got to the post where the coats had been hung, my donkey jacket had gone but another one was left there. I was now the last client in the pub and that was the last coat so I grabbed it, put it on and walked home nestled inside its comfortable warmth. When I got home I examined the coat in more detail and found that I had traded up. I had had a regular donkey jacket, not a crap one but one of the good ones. This, however, was top shelf.

Donkey jackets were workingmen's jackets made of a thick black warm material with leather on the shoulders to keep the rain off. Cheap versions had plastic on the shoulders. The one I had acquired at the Kings Head, however, had leather on the shoulders but it also went all the way down the back. This was unusual and good, as it made the jacket extra sturdy and extra rain resistant without sacrificing warmth.

There I was at the party in Fulham with my unusually acquired donkey jacket when a young Englishman named Josh introduced himself and asked about my jacket. I told him how I got it. Josh said that the jacket was his. He had been drunk that night at the Kings Head and must have accidentally picketed up my donkey jacket. We agreed this one was better and unusually good. I really expected Josh to ask for the jacket and I think he would have done if he had my old one with him but he didn't so he didn't. He put his reduced circumstances down to fate and mismanagement, and let things be. I've always thought his action magnanimous.

Larry, Trout and I talked and laughed and drank and carried on for a few hours before the party died and the beer ran out; these two events being more or less simultaneous. Jolly after an unexpectedly good evening, we headed back to Halford Road. The night was cold and still and we thoroughly enjoyed the walk. I know I did. We had completely forgotten about the stew but remembered it on the way home, and remembered we were hungry. We began to hasten on the frozen ground and through the misty air. We had barely turned into Halford Road and were still a couple of hundred metres from home when we smelt the curried rabbit stew. Now we really hurried; excited in an anticipation that was mixed with fear about what we might find.

When we opened the front door the aroma poured out of the house. The smell was great. We rushed down the hall to the kitchen and curried rabbit stew. The liquid had reduced, the vegetables dissolved, and the meat just fallen off the bones leaving the whole thing absolutely prime. We were just at the point where if it had been any later it would have started to burn but now it was perfect and we were starving.

The Blockheads

Ian Drury has gone…rest his weary soul. He died too young in 2000, but he was a great performer. We, however, didn't give him the respect he deserved and it was our own loss.

One afternoon Peter Lowe turned up at the Halford Road squat with some speed. He also had money and insisted that we all go to see Ian Drury and the Blockheads play over in north London. I think it was somewhere in Islington. This was pretty much a last minute offer, brought on by who knows what, but we couldn't refuse. So after a solid line of speed we headed off.

Normally, if we were going to pay to see a band we would go to see the whole show, including all of the support acts, but on this occasion we got there just as the headline act launched onto the stage. The Blockheads seemed to be playing well, and I tried to appreciate the music and the performance, but I was out of rhythm. It was a waste all round. If, rather than amphetamines, we had smoked some grass and/or had a few drinks, I'm sure the show would have been great, but it had been spoilt by the demanding energy of the speed.

Ambulance

One night Larry, Trout and I were walking back to Fulham, drunk and wired up on something or other. An ambulance was parked in the street looking spacey with its lights on but no one in it. Some idiot — it was me — suggested that we take the ambulance for a spin. Fortunately someone else thought better of it. Later, we were so grateful that we had not been THAT stupid.

Gaffney and Heaven

When Trout, Larry and I had been living at Halford Road for a few of months, our mate Gaffney arrived in London. He was one of Larry and my closest friends from Burra. While he was a little disappointed with our less than salubrious accommodation, Gaffney moved straight in.

Gaffney arrived with a commodity that was in very short supply for the rest of us, money, and he was a keen musician so our band watching activities received a sudden and significant boost. We started to go to see more local bands and even some of the bigger bands that came to London. At the time, many of the better known visiting bands of the kind that most interested us would play at a venue called 'Heaven', which was under the arches at Charing Cross. The performances at Heaven were beyond our means but Gaffney was enthusiastic and paid our entries so we could hardly refuse.

Heaven had a variety of areas from which you could watch bands, or ignore them if you preferred. The large room where the bands performed provided for the traditional mosh pit in front of the stage but there were several other rooms including a kind of glassed mezzanine bar overlooking that area. Presumably, this layout was designed to allow patrons to watch the dance floor action below because the six days of the week when it was not a venue for bands Heaven was a gay nightclub.

Heaven may have changed into a performance space for alternative rock outfits one day per week but the staff remained the same. It was slightly surreal going to see post-punk bands and being served drinks by little party boys in shortie pink satin shorts with neat, tight, white singlets.

We saw some very good bands at Heaven in what seemed to be an especially innovative era. The standout performance, I think we all agreed, was by Pere Ubu.

Heaven used to go late by London's standards and the tube would have already stopped running by the time we left. More than once we found ourselves on the lengthy walk back to Fulham, still running on the adrenalin produced by the bands' performance.

Brighton Jethro Tull

Having tired of the regular London delights, Gaffney, Trout, Larry and I decided to head off for Brighton. Why we four Halford Road residents decided on Brighton I don't know but I suppose that it was the most famous of the English seaside towns and it was close to London.

The map said that the distance from London to Brighton was fifty odd miles. Where I come from, that would have meant a journey of just under an hour. I wasn't expecting that but I was still surprised how long the whole thing took.

Once we got to Brighton we had no idea what we were going to do. Apart from the beach, there were no sights that I was anticipating seeing and I think that was also the case for Trout, Gaffney and Larry. We had not planned one second of the journey beyond the train trip so as soon as we alighted from the train we set out in search of tourist information in order to find some accommodation.

There is a saying about having to say hello if you see someone three times and this is what happened to us. Wandering in a disorderly fashion in the general direction of away, we were looking for a sign with an 'i' symbol when we saw this guy who looked superficially not unlike the flute player from Jethro Tull. You would have noticed him anywhere with his unusual and colourful clothes and his long hair and platted beard but to make himself even more conspicuous he was carrying a large camera and tripod. We observed him as we sauntered past and then we turned the next corner and walked along a little and came across him again. Shortly after this we decided that we must be going in the wrong direction so we turned around and headed more of less back from where we had come and soon enough we came across the same distinctive figure. This being the third time, we sort of had to acknowledge each other's existence.

'What are you looking for?' asked the photographer. 'The tourist information', one of us replied. 'Yes, but what are you looking for', he reiterated. Doing our best impression of ignorant know-nothing tourists, we restated our objective in the same terms. Eventually, however, we realised what he was asking and told him that we were looking for somewhere to stay. He said that we could stay at his place. He told us his address but warned us that he would not be there until sometime that evening.

'Great', we thought, and headed off to take in the sights of Brighton. This consisted of going down to the beach and, like generations of Australians before us, being disappointed that the beach was covered in white gravel. Swimming was clearly not an option and what with one thing and another we ended up in a pub.

Somewhere about the time that we should have left to take up the kindly-offered free digs, the level of alcohol in our systems kicked beyond the ability to make sensible decisions so we carried on drinking, playing pool, laughing and generally having a good time. This continued until stumps when we found ourselves outside the pub with very little option but to go around to the photographer's place and hope for the best.

I wasn't sure that we even had the address right but we knocked on the door and after a little while our friend appeared and let us in. This guy was the exemplum of exotic hospitality. We sat around for a little while in his odd but fascinating house surrounded by books, art and artefacts. He made us drinks and found sleeping quarters for us. We were completely undeserving but he fulfilled his generous offer.

The next morning the Ian Anderson lookalike provided breakfast and asked us to stay. We had blown all the money that we had for the trip and said that we would head back to London. Why we did that I will never know. I had nothing of any value back in the capital. I certainly didn't have a job and I can only but wonder about how things would have worked out had we, or I, stayed longer in this great place with this interesting character. But, like the urban flotsam we had become, we sailed back to the familiarity of Halford Road.

The sack of potatoes

One quiet morning, Trout, Larry, Gaffney and I were sitting around in Halford Road when Peter Lowe burst in carrying a 50 pound sack of potatoes. Apparently, he just happened to be walking along North End Road not far from the corner of Halford Road when he noticed that the stallholder was distracted. Peter Lowe simply hoisted the sack onto his shoulder and kept walking up to our squat.

So, there we are sitting around in a super-cosy kitchen just before noon when Peter Lowe rocks in with his huge sack of potatoes. He sits down has a cup of tea and a quick chat and then heads off giving some vague indication that he might see us that afternoon or evening.

How lucky are we? We soon settled into a kind of creative cooking exercise heavily based on the noble spud. Initially we simply went through our limited repertoire of potato cooking: boiled, baked, chipped and mashed. After we had explored those options in a variety of orders we started to get a touch more adventurous. Boiled potatoes could then be fried, to give then a nice oily crust. Mashed potato cookery turned out to be its own world of renewed opportunities. The mash would be rolled into balls and fried or backed, or flattened mash balls could be grilled with a little butter. If the whole bonanza had gone on for long enough I'm sure that we would have progressed from this second order (that is, 'postmodern') cookery to some third order constructions.

One of the reasons that sort of creative variation didn't happen was that we had some help with the ingestion of the spuds. Word soon spread in our little squat-centred circle that we possessed a superabundance of potatoes. Squat world of necessity is a bit of a share world, and stolen things are not as owned as legally obtained ones. We could hardly deny the requests when visitors came around, so soon enough a spud would be boiling away.

A couple named Robert and Amy lived in a squat about half a dozen doors along Halford Road toward North End Road. I don't know how they got by but they weren't overly cashed up. They quickly formed the habit of dropping around very frequently; it seemed like every day and probably was. When they turned up, the veneer of polite conversation was more or less translucently thin and almost immediately the discussion would turn to potatoes. Then Robert and Amy would be cooking up some ignoble spuds in our cosy kitchen. We liked the company.

Mainz and Wiesbaden

My money was effectively gone, the money Larry had saved in Germany was almost gone, and Gaffney's money was going. Larry still had connections in Wiesbaden and convinced us that we could get better paid work over there, possibly on a building site. The three of us booked a bus ticket to Amsterdam thinking that we would make our way from there down to the German region of Frankfurt Rhine Main.

This was another Magic Bus trip so naturally I was a little nervous but the journey was uneventful and in Amsterdam we checked in to a little terrace house that had been converted into a tiny hostel. The great number of bicycles, the daily marches through the centre of town where we were, and the better quality of food were the things that most struck me about the Dutch city. Naturally we enjoyed the café culture where every coffee shop seemed to have a resident hash dealer and we went along to the Melkweg to see the bands and to experience the novelty of the open purchase of different varieties of cannabis, which simply had their names and prices written on a blackboard.

We had no set time to be in Amsterdam and would have stayed longer than just a couple of days but on the evening of the second day another resident of the hostel offered us a lift. Klaus, an Austrian who occasionally worked in Holland, said he was leaving the next day and he could give us a ride down into Germany.

140

The following morning we loaded ourselves and our packs into Klaus's car for the trip south. We had only made it a couple of streets from the hostel though when Klaus drove up onto the footpath, where he put a tourniquet on his arm and quickly hit himself up with some speed, I think. This was all a bit of a shock. We knew people who used drugs but this public performance was something new.

Klaus had a BMW and once we hit the Dutch equivalent of the autobahn we really motored along. The main problem seemed to be navigation as Klaus didn't see so well for a short while after he hit up and as we lurched towards major junctions it was up to us passengers to tell him what the signs said. This only seemed to be an issue in the Netherlands, once we got into Germany he knew where he was going; maybe the drugs had settled down.

Hurtling down the motorway I was surprised to see a car racing up behind us. It was the Dutch highway patrol and they were driving a high performance Porsche cabriolet. The police slowed long enough to pause briefly beside our vehicle where one of them stood up in the open cockpit and indicated to us that we shouldn't go any faster before the Porsche shot away ahead of us. The display was impressive but it also had a comical element as the policeman stood in a slightly ungainly way, challenged by the wind, and seemed to be wearing a leather helmet and goggles, so the act had a touch of both Biggles and Inspector Clouseau.

When we arrived at the German border there was slight hitch as Klaus had a large clear plastic bag full of some kind of dried green leaf. We hoped it wasn't pot and customs questioned it but Klaus explained that it was some kind of herbal remedy and they seemed to be happy.

Germany is big. It included enormous industrial zones that were very new to me. Essen, which I hadn't even heard of, was a gigantic urban and industrial sprawl. When I consulted a map I realised that several cites had grown to the point where they had merged into one.

We seemed to drive for a long time. As the evening was approaching we started to wonder where we would spend the night but Klaus said not to worry as he could find us a place. It was already dark when we got to Dusseldorf and Klaus pulled off the autobahn and onto a local road. After a short drive, he took us to some kind of youth centre that had accommodation for many more people than were staying there at the time and they were happy for us to stay the night.

The following morning Klaus drove on to Köln and that's where he left us. We took time out to walk around the cathedral before we strode up to the Köln *Hauptbahnhof* and purchased rail tickets to Frankfurt. After a little time in Frankfurt, which struck me more as a functional city than an inspiring one, we bought tickets to Mainz, which is where we were going to stay even though we would be mainly looking for work in Wiesbaden. Both Mainz and Wiesbaden were near enough to Frankfurt to be on its local rail network.

In Mainz we checked into a large old hotel almost opposite the *Hauptbahnhof.* The rooms were not that big but they were comfortable enough and the place was surprisingly cheap.

While we were in Mainz, a local mentioned to us that it was a very historic town. We accepted what he said but had no idea how historic it was. It was only later that I discovered that it had been a Roman city and then the home of the Prince-elector of Mainz during the Holy Roman Empire, and it was there that Gutenberg introduced the printing press to Europe and invented movable type. It was also much later that I found out that there are Chagall stain glass windows in St. Stephan's church which was only a few minutes from the hotel.

Larry's friends were in Wiesbaden. Most were Americans who worked for the US base there. I got the impression that Wiesbaden was a larger and more modern city than Mainz. For me, Wiesbaden's main point of difference was the large number of American service people there. As we walked around the streets we would often come across groups of soldiers or other military personnel walking the streets. It was quickly very clear that a disproportionate number of coloured people are in the US military forces.

There were so many US servicepeople in Wiesbaden that US Military Police patrolled the streets. Individual armed MPs would wander around like Bobbies on the beat. One day we noticed that a single young MP was being followed by an even younger German teenager. The girl was just far enough behind the MP for the casual observer not to notice that they were really a pair walking around together, only several metres apart.

One evening Larry, Gaffney and I were sitting in the beer garden of a Wiesbaden hotel where steaks and other meals were served. We were seated at a long wooden table on a bench seat and most of the others at the table were Americans. Directly opposite me was a US serviceman and beside him was his German girlfriend. A waiter brought out the steak that the soldier had ordered. It was an enormous rib steak about an inch thick with a neat cylinder of garlic butter on top. There was also a fresh salad and a healthy serve of chips on the large plate. The whole thing looked very inviting, especially for someone who was not that flush.

No sooner had the waiter put the plated steak on the table than the German woman snaffled one of her boyfriend's chips. This led to a loud and protracted argument. The serviceman said that he could not eat anything once his food had been touched. He argued that she may as well eat the meal because there was no way that he could have it now. She said that she had not meant any harm, she had only taken one chip, and the rest was completely untouched so he should eat it without any concern. He would not budge and she was insistent that she could not eat his meal.

As this storm raged I was sitting directly opposite, appreciating the beautiful, and effectively pristine, meal that was right in front of me. When the argument had ground to a halt and the two protagonists were sitting there in quiet huffs, I asked, 'Can I have it?' 'Go ahead', said the soldier. So I did. It was delicious. I enjoyed every mouthful of that juicy steak, that lovely fresh salad and those crisp tasty chips.

Over the next couple of weeks, Larry was preoccupied looking up old friends and hunting down a job so Gaffney and I were largely left to our own devices. We were often back and forth between Mainz and Wiesbaden on the train and we got into the habit of not paying for our tickets. One time when we did this, two ticket inspectors got onto the train at one of the lesser stations. Surprised, we discretely slid away along the carriage and alighted at the next stop. Standing on the platform of this bleakish station we wondered what it was doing there. We were grateful, however, that it had saved our bacon.

While Larry was off looking for a job or just catching up with his friends in Wiesbaden, Gaffney and I took to sleeping in and getting up about lunchtime when we would go around to Rimini's Italian restaurant, where the food was excellent. We went there about five days in a row and that was enough to get us onto the specials list. The very first day the list was shown to us it included a dish called Rigatoni alla Arrabiata. I had never heard of it and the waiter explained the name by saying, 'I am angry, I want to fight you'. I gathered that it was a fiery dish and ordered it.

The pasta that arrived had a sublimely simple tomato, garlic, chilli and basil sauce. It was divine. I ate the lot and then cleaned the plate with the bread. When I had finished there was no visible sign that the plate had ever been contaminated by food. The waiter came to collect the plate and laughed. Then he went out to the kitchen and told the chef, Marco, that I had complained about the dish. Marco stormed out to confront the insulting customer only to be shown the clean plate and also laugh. I thanked him and he thanked me and then he adjourned back to the kitchen. From then on Gaffney and I referred to him as 'Marco, god of pasta'.

Mainz is one of the main German cities where the festival of *Fasching* is celebrated and we happened to be there during the event. We all made ourselves up for the occasion, putting various colours on out faces. Gaffney said that Larry and I we looked like Kiss impersonators. Gaffney himself was a bit of a thespian and so much more skilled in the dramatic arts, including make up; he looked like a bluish zombie.

The parade was fun and it was also enjoyable going from hotel to hotel. Virtually every bar seemed to have its own fully operational oompah band going flat out with absolutely everyone joining it. Being made up, we were welcomed wherever we went, but we were not equipped to sing along.

Larry looked like getting some work in Wiesbaden but Gaffney and I did not. This, it must be said, was probably more a result of our almost complete lack of effort than it was the fact that we had not worked there before and had little or no experience on building sites.

For Gaffney and I, the trip had degenerated into a lazy, gourmet farce, and in short time it was over. I'd been all but broke to begin with and the money that Gaffney had brought had been frittered away on accommodation, alcohol and good food. Our prospects in Germany seemed to be limited and we weren't making an effort. When it got down to the point that there was just enough money for return fares for the two of us we headed off leaving Larry there with his friends and job prospects.

Initially, Gaffney and I didn't get very far. In fact the first leg of our journey took us only as far as the Frankfurt Railway Station and the next train to Belgium did not leave until the next morning. We tried to sleep in the waiting room of the Frankfurt, *Hauptbahnhof* but every hour these large chunky chaps in green uniforms — I'm guessing they were some kind of police — moved us on. We were left with nothing to do but to spend the small hours walking around Frankfurt until we could stay back at the station. We had to walk because it was too cold to sit still outside.

The following day we boarded the train, which eventually took us to Ostend where we boarded the ferry for Ramsgate. The journey was reasonably quick but it was an ordeal nevertheless.

When we finally made it onto the ferry we were exhausted. We crashed soon after departure and slept till the ferry had docked at Ramsgate, and then we were still so tired that we were very slow to get moving. Consequently, we were the very last two passengers to alight. This in itself is probably suspicious but when added to our dishevelled appearance, bells would have been going off in the minds of the officials that we had to please.

Sure enough, Customs decided to give us a thorough going over. Everything was emptied and then dismantled. Our few paltry possessions, however, hid nothing but the fact that there wasn't anything else. Disappointed, customs sent us on to Immigration who were standing around bored. They asked us the most basic of questions before putting the standard twelve month working visas in our passports. No one had noticed that we had no money; in my case not a single p. We made our way down to the railway platform but the connecting train was long gone. An hour or two later, however, we were back on our way to the English capital.

Kentish Town

Gaffney and I had only been back at Halford Road for a couple of weeks when our little world was shaken. The building we occupied in Halford Road was owned by a community housing group and it was going to be refurbished. They advised us that, after the appropriate time, they would be taking possession and the builders would move in. We took note of this advice but there were differing levels of response to it.

Larry had only arrived back a couple of days prior to us receiving the notice and he was keen to return to Germany as he was convinced that his prospects were going to be realised over there, and Gaffney decided to go with him. The two of them set out to return to Wiesbaden the following week.

To the best of my knowledge, Trout didn't do anything about our impending homelessness but I began discussing the situation with Gerry Tunk. Gerry was staying with an old friend from Rhodesia named Donald, who had a bedsit in Kentish Town. Gerry was temporarily occupying the lounge and he wanted to find a roomier venue. We agreed that I would come around to the bedsit the following Monday morning.

When the day dawned, for me, I was completely skint. If I had any money at all it was less than 20p. Given the lack of cash, I would usually have caught the tube and just have done a runner but I needed to go to a station and an area I didn't know so I thought it prudent to acquire a fare. A couple of days before I had been in the Robert and Amy's squat just half a dozen doors along Halford Road and had noticed that there were some coins in the gas meter. Their place was owned by the same housing organisation that was about to take possession of our house and Robert and Amy had already been evicted. I thought that the money would probably still be in the gas meter. So, as soon as I got up I walked down the street determined to ill-get the strong-boxed pittance.

I was confident of getting into the house but whoever had secured it after the departure of Robert and Amy had done a good job and I couldn't open the front door or the window on the ground floor. Full of anxiety, I climbed the front of the house aided by the small tree in the front yard. Standing on the ledge of the first floor window, trying to jemmy it open, and hoping no one across the street would look out, I noticed a policeman wandering along the Halford Road.

With nothing but the spindly black branches of the leafless sapling between me and exposure, I just had to stand there, clinging to the window and hope the bobby wouldn't look up. He didn't. He passed by with his head just two metres from my feet. If he had glanced to his left I would have been like a deer in a spotlight.

The situation was beyond urgent now and as soon as the policeman had wandered a few doors along I started to try to force the window and managed to get in. Little did I know what the scenario that had been played out was only the vestibule of a very difficult day with the law.

Once I had got into the house, the next challenge was the meter box. It was a battle but, eventually, I managed to open it using only the few useless bits of rubbish lying around and brute force. The dream was probably of a pound or two but I got only a few pence more than the minimum fare. By 'minimum fare' I mean I was in the habit of riding the tube and when I arrived at my destination I would announce the name of the previous station and give the ticket collector the fare for a one-stop journey. Having got to the strange because new to me, but pleasant enough, London station of Kentish Town, I did just that. Then I found my way to the bedsit where Gerry was staying. He was the only one home. He sat me down and cracked out some pot — grass from Rhodesia.

He was still rolling the joint when, suddenly, there were several other people in the room. One hint of a glance at these strangers told us they were police or similar — probably drug or vice squad or something like that. Whatever they were, they were from some government authority and extremely unwelcome. I later learnt that it was a joint operation of several groups including the police and customs, and they had a skeleton key or some such thing.

While shocked by the sudden appearance of these men, something along these lines had been a possibility in my life for some time. Taking in the scene, I was very impressed with how quickly Gerry disposed of the grass and paraphernalia so almost instantly there was a room full of men but no pot in sight.

A couple of the men got Gerry and I to empty our pockets and what not. Then they questioned us in situ while others went about searching the flat in a violent and ruthless manner.

We were interviewed simultaneously and I was trying to listen to Gerry while answering the questions I was being asked. I couldn't take in much of what Gerry was saying as I was being interviewed but my story was surprisingly honest. Making no mention of my activities earlier that morning, I told the police I had come around to see Gerry because we planned to get new, shared accommodation. I later learnt that they assumed I was a petty grass consumer and had come around to score.

At one point during these proceedings, Gerry asked to relieve himself. While he was off doing so there was a sort of new mini-commotion that brought, for the first time, a few uniformed police into the flat.

149

Somehow Gerry had managed to keep the joint he was rolling hidden in his hand or hidden somewhere on him. When he went to the toilet he tossed the smoke out the window. The way he told the story, the police were waiting out there and caught the joint before rushing in with the news and their prize.

Then the search resumed in a more orderly, but no less violent, fashion. This is true, one of the policemen who was now involved in the search really did froth at the mouth; just a little, but enough.

While this was going on we were made to sit back down. We had nothing to do to contain our nervous energy so we chain-smoked, interrupting the constant stream of lung-busters with the odd puff on Gerry's Ventolin.

Given that there had been quite a bit of grass in the room when the authorities burst in, the search took a surprisingly long time to produce anything but the joint we had been about to smoke. One of the first things that had been overturned in the too-excited search was the cupboard under which Gerry had kicked the block of compressed cannabis. I had seen it there but the frantic furniture rearrangement had actually concealed the pot even better.

During what was probably a period of only about fifteen or twenty minutes, but seemed much longer, the search went on in a clearly frustrated way; they had the joint but this operation had much bigger fish to fry. Soon enough, however, they found the pound or two of marijuana and the scales behind the cupboard lying on its back. The search carried on after this but they had what they needed and now they were happy. We were asked to explain the presence of the block of cannabis and obviously we couldn't.

The police assumed that the drugs belonged to Gerry and others, but not me, as they did not press me too hard but clearly didn't believe him. We were given some more formal questions and warnings before they marched us outside.

As I was going out I surveyed the room. From what I could see there was not one piece of furniture nor a single fitting that was in place. Everything was on its side, pulled up, pulled down, or pushed over and strewn about the room.

Gerry and I were put into separate police cars in front of a few scattered and vaguely curious spectators. There were many more police and representatives of other agencies than there were casual viewers. Then we were driven off to the local police station and put into the cells.

I had been in a police cell before in Kensington so when a meal was offered I took the chance even though I recognised it for the small, tepid, tasteless and textureless version of a roast that it was. You had to have lived a little to recognise the vegetables. On the basis of my Kensington Police Station experience, I also accepted the watery, and equally tepid, tea when it was offered. Then I tried to exercise because I was experiencing my first real bout of claustrophobia. I've hated cells ever since.

Every hour while I was in there a policeman would come around and look through the little window latches of the cells and ask the residents for some acknowledgement. After a few hours, each round of this routine included numerous shouts of 'Purvis? Purvis! Purvis!!'

It turns out that this Purvis was the guy I knew as Donald. His day had been worse than mine. Tripping on acid, he had returned home to his flat where Gerry was staying. Opening the door Purvis was confronted by one of his worst nightmares. Inside the flat were several policemen who were waiting for him. They grabbed him, interviewed him, and then carted him off to the same police cells where Gerry and I were now residents.

I can only imagine what Purvis's state of mind was like as he occupied his compact personal dungeon a few doors from my own. Clearly, he was not responding promptly to the hourly check and this is why his name was being yelled repeatedly each time. At the time, however, I didn't know that Purvis was Donald's surname so I didn't know he was in there.

151

About three in the morning the police decided I was surplus to requirements. They gave me back my few pence and whatever else I had — probably some rollies — and directed me to the door. As this was my first trip to this part of town and to this police station it took me a little while to get organised and work out where I was going on that cold night. Eventually I found my way back to the flat which was about half a mile away.

When I got to the terrace another ex-pat named Andrew was there. He was either South African or Rhodesian and it was him that filled me in on poor Purvis's unhappy experience. Andrew told me that some friend in Africa had been posting over grass a few pounds at a time. It seemed likely that customs had intercepted a shipment and then sent it on. My new acquaintance then asked me if I wanted to smoke some pot. Extremely nervously, I said, 'Sure.'

The room had been tidied up a little since I left. Most of the furniture was more or less back in its place and standing up but no effort had been made to repair the fixtures. Sometimes things are invisible even to the most professional and enthusiastic horde of searchers. That's the only way that I can explain what happened next.

Andrew went over to the gas heater. It was one of those little ones that sit on the floor but are fixed to the wall. He pulled the heater away from the wall. Behind it was a solid block of grass; at least a couple of pounds of that dark, really resinous, African stuff that was the cause of all the commotion.

We rolled a skinny joint and smoked it while looking out the window every few seconds. This was an excruciating experience and my paranoia was off the dial. We smoked the joint Afrikaans style. You smoke it down to a tiny little butt, then roll the butt into a ball and burn it, snorting the smoke as you do so. We had several of these and cups of tea until daylight. Then I headed back to Fulham.

Kentish Town: Postscript 1

There's a kind of afterword that should go with that day. While Gerry and Donald had a contact in Zimbabwe who was sending them grass purchased from local indigenous Africans, there was a sort of parallel operation conducted by some South African acquaintances of theirs. This affair began before that day at Kentish Town and finished after it. The method was simple and might be called suitcase lotto.

According to the SAS motto, fortune favours the brave and that can be how it seems. Remembering that this was the olden days at the beginning of the eighties, the first guy simply filled a suitcase with powerful African heads — it might have been 'Durban poison' — and boarded a plane to London. On the proceeds, there he lived a sort of low-life high-life of smoking pot, drinking and socialising. The next guy did the same thing with the same result. And so it went on to the fifth guy who was captured at Heathrow with his suitcase full of grass. I imagine he was incapable of explaining the presence of the drugs.

Whether the authorities had some intelligence or they simply got lucky at customs, no one knew.

Kentish Town: Postscript 2

The joint operation at Kentish Town wasn't the best drug raid that I saw in London but I was just an accidental spectator in the other one; by which I mean that I didn't know any of the personnel involved.

The best bust I saw was a sudden and violent assault on a couple of thirty-something men in either Earls Court Gardens or Barksten Gardens Street, about the same distance off Earls Court Road as the Kings Head was a street or two away. I just happened to be walking along on the opposite footpath when a car pulled up and these two guys got out. The vehicle was probably a cab but I was not paying any attention as these men two alighted but the moment they did they were descended upon. This was clearly a heavy-duty action as it involved weapons and undercover police.

What really struck me about that scene, and intensified its impact and memorability, was that up to that point in time hardly anyone outside of inner west London had heard of a 'Sloane Ranger' but one of the undercover guys was about six foot three and had pink hair. He was one of the first and best Sloane Rangers I ever saw and he wasn't even a real one. When I think back on the sudden and powerful action with that athletic tall young guy and his bright pink hair, Michael Moorcock's Jerry Cornelius comes to mind…not that there is any real connection.

Our abrupt departure from Halford Road

The ill-fated expedition to see Gerry Tunk was my one attempt to find new digs and it had been wildly unsuccessful. After that I had become distracted and if the looming accommodation crisis had not actually slipped my mind then it had certainly receded to some of its darker recesses.

This might seem hard to believe, but the day came when Trout and I were woken from our slumber and our lackadaisical haze by a young building worker smashing down the front door. Having nearly forgotten our impending eviction, we were both sound asleep when startled by this extremely violent start to the day and didn't know what had happened until we raced out to where the front was caved in to find the cause. I still see Trout lurching past my door as I was making my way toward the violent commotion.

The young guy was apologetic but there was no need to be as the situation was completely of our making. We accepted our fate and packed up the few most treasured and transportable belongings and headed off we knew not where.

Pellant Road and Catweazle

No sooner had we been evicted than Trout had himself a new home. Robert and Amy who had been in the squat several doors down Halford Road toward the market, and who so enjoyed our potatoes, had found themselves another habitable abode just around the corner. They were now set up in a little terrace in Knivett Road. Robert and Amy were the nearest people that we knew and we carried our few belonging straight around there immediately after the builders smashed their way into our place. The pair were both real softies and when we asked to leave the gear there they offered Trout the lounge if he needed it. He accepted without hesitation.

Once again I was left homeless but this time there was a solution just a few streets away. Robert and Amy told us that Gerry Tunk was now in a squat at 14 Pellant Road, which was just two or three streets the other side of North End Road. I went around to see if there was a spare room and was delighted to find that there were several and I was welcome to one. I walked back around to Knivett Road, collected by things, and then moved right in.

The house at 14 Pellant Road was a three story white terrace on the end of the street opposite to what I assume were large blocks of council flats. Gerry lived in the basement flat with a South African guy who had that indeterminate age look, but presumably was about thirty. Everyone called him Catweazle. I never knew his real name but one of his mates once referred to him as 'Old Reg'.

Catweazle spent almost the entirety of every day sitting in a beanbag in the middle of the downstairs lounge room watching TV. He was almost like a fixture. No doubt, this extreme lethargy was partially a product of Catweazle's physical make up but it was facilitated by his use of heroin. Wherever he possibly could, which was a lot, he sat there stoned watching TV.

Once in operation, however, Catweazle could be single-minded, quick and ruthless. He was a very adept thief. His favourite targets seemed to be electronic goods. One day Catweazle, Gerry and I were walking past a shop that sold electronic appliances. Catweazle abruptly stopped and announced that he would just have a quick peek inside. He seemed to have barely entered the shop when he discretely shot back out again. Under his coat was a huge ghetto blaster. We hastened away. I was incredulous on several fronts. Why pick such a large thing? And how could he pick it up, wrap his coat around it and leave without anyone noticing?

Frank Chappell

There were three rooms on the top floor of the squat at 14 Pellant Road and two of these rooms were empty. I moved into the middle one. Frank Chappell, who I already knew, lived in the front room.

I'm not sure when I first met Frank but it must have been about a year or so before we ended up sharing the same floor at the Pellant Road squat in Fulham. When I first met him, Frank worked for a casual work agency somewhere around Earls Court. He was a gentle and generous soul and he used to drive the van that would take him and his fellow workers to wherever the job was. Since then, his circumstances had been suddenly and greatly reduced. Frank already had some history so when the excrement had hit the fan there had been no safety net.

One day, for whatever reason, the van that Frank was driving to work was pulled over by the police. When the police checked they found that his licence had expired. To make matters worse, they discovered that he was collecting the dole while he was driving the work van. He lost his job and he lost his social security. Frank had nothing.

Frank had a variety of problems and dependencies, and these are what he would exploit to keep himself going. When you take a lot of speed you tend to get very anxious, especially when the speed is wearing off. At times like that, you really need some help.

Valium was sometimes prescribed to take a little weight off and to ease users through the dreadful blackness.

With the help of a compliant doctor, Frank turned his co-dependencies into a survival mechanism. Every week he would get a script for 60 Duromine and 60 Valium (the big ones of both). Duromine were diet pills that are also strong stimulants. They were taken recreationally — misused if you prefer — as speed. Frank would take the Duromine that he was prescribed and sell the Valium. Given that his rate was very much bargain basement — 6 to 10 Valium per £1 — that would leave Frank with about six or seven pounds to live on for the week. From what I recall, he virtually ate nothing but drank some tea and smoked rollies.

So, Frank had a weekly cycle and it went pretty much like this. When he first collected his prescription, he would start taking the Duromine and be on a high. The window in Frank's room on the top floor of the squat was directly over the front door. Frank was constantly standing at that window looking out. If Catweazle was a fixture in his beanbag in front of the TV downstairs, Frank's role overlooking the doorway was a bit like that of a gargoyle on a church.

The Duromine made Frank hallucinate. At the start of the cycle, he would be at the window looking out and he would see exciting things like a couple groping in a car parked at the front of the house or making love in a room across the road. There was a lot of sex in this early phase. 'Come on, come on, come and look at this', he would say. I would drag myself over fully expecting to find that the things that Frank thought he could see were not there. Then, when I looked I would see that the hot sexual action was really the play of shadow from the tree in the street on the window across the road, or something similar. This first part of the cycle was the high and it lasted for a day or so.

Frank wouldn't sleep for days at a time while he was taking the Duromine and the hallucinations would get worse as the cycle progressed. The excitement of nude babes and hot raunchy action would be replaced by threatening characters lurking in the street or even looking into Frank's first floor window. Then the diet pills (taken as speed) would run out. This would be the time when Frank really needed to take the Valium to ease him through the horror but the pills had gone to provide for all his other needs, apart from the roof over his head.

How he coped through the final day or two of each cycle I don't know but he would collapse for at least some part of the time as it is not possible to continue week after week without any sleep. It goes without saying that Frank would really need that Duromine by the time he got the next week's script.

Frank was still trapped in this cycle when I left London but later I heard that the police had picked him up for some misdemeanour. That would have been exactly what he needed because, after paying his debt to society, Frank would have the slate wiped clean so he could at least get the dole again. Although, in my opinion, what he needed was some kind of disability pension and proper — not overly generous — medical help.

A bottle of scotch from Sainsbury's

I've really got no explanation for this one. I don't know what I was thinking. I don't know if there was a party or something so that I felt some special need to have a supply of alcohol or it was just a case of hubris. It may well have been some kind of vanity rising out of my chronic success stealing steaks from the mini supermarket in Earls Court, but I went down to the Sainsbury's in North End Road with the intention of stealing a bottle of scotch.

I should have expected that there would be greater security around the alcohol but, if anything, I was even more lax and stupid than usual. I wandered around the shop looking at the security while giving the impression of shopping for this item or that. I had been into the shop several times before but I always did a lap as I checked things out. Then I went to the drink section, picked up the bottle, made one more extremely quick furtive glance and stuffed it up under my coat.

As I did so I thought a woman might have noticed me but I wasn't sure. I don't know why I persisted because never before had I done so when I thought that someone might have seen me, and this was bound to be a more closely guarded item. Nevertheless, I carried on in my usual manner of stealing from shops.

As I approached the checkout, queued up and went through I felt very uneasy. All I needed to do was to take the bottle out before I left the shop, but I didn't. So, after paying for some tiny item, as I did as a way of justifying my shopping outing, I walked as casually as I could to and through the front door. As I turned right onto the footpath I was confronted by two store employees. I immediately shot off diagonally left through the traffic on North End Road and towards the intersection of Eustace Road. As I reached the footpath another employee came running towards me from my left. I have never played Rugby or Rugby League but my left hand shot out and he was gone; it was the palm off of a lifetime. The action and the necessary change in direction it involved had slowed me down a little and one of the two men who had confronted me when I first left the store were now very close to me on my right hand side. I tried to sprint along the footpath on the left but I didn't get very far before one of the pursuers got hold of my coat and then they were all on me.

Not long after I was jumped on, two policemen turned up in a small paddy wagon and I was loaded inside. The Sainsbury's employees were insisting that I would be charged with shoplifting and assault, claiming that I had punched the guy who confronted me as I crossed North End Road, but I was adamant that I had just put my hand out to stop him as he hurtled toward me.

I was taken to Fulham Police Station and put into the cells, and left there for a few hours. While I was in a cell by myself and the usual claustrophobia was coming on, the experience was reasonably entertaining as that afternoon Chelsea was playing at home and one loud and drunken football hooligan after another was checked into our temporary holding facility. I don't remember any of the remarks but there were plenty and they ranged from the incomprehensible through the stupid to the humorous and even on to the witty.

Maybe it was the influx of soccer louts or maybe the police were giving me some time to stew but I seemed to be left in the cell for a much longer time that was necessary given the straightforward circumstances.

The police seem to have decided that it was going to be too hard to get the conviction for the assault and given that the bottle stealing was an open and shut case they would go with that. So I was sent off secure in the knowledge that I would have to appear in court in the near future.

Sure enough, a few weeks later I found myself facing a magistrate in court. I was charged with stealing the bottle of scotch and I pleaded guilty. There wasn't much else to it and when I was asked if I had anything to say I basically pleaded poverty and an aberration. I was fined. It wasn't very much, £10 or £20 I think, but it was certainly more than I had and I was given some time to pay.

While I was in court I saw that the woman who I thought had noticed me slipping the bottle under my coat was there watching proceedings. No doubt she was a store detective. As soon as I was convicted and fined she got up and left the public section of the court.

The day I nearly hit up; or, why I've never used drugs intravenously

Gaffney and Larry's return trip to Germany had not been the great success that they had anticipated and it seemed that they were hardly gone from London before they were back again. Apparently, almost everything they did to try to get to Wiesbaden was hindered or went wrong in one way or another, but the moment they gave up and decided to head back to London everything went uncannily well. Quickly they found us in Pellant Road where there were rooms to spare so they moved straight in.

Everyone in the basement flat of the squat had been using heroin for some time but of the upstairs residents, Gaffney and I had only smoked or snorted it. Seemingly sensibly, on what we thought of as a kind of economically rational basis, we decided that we would hit up the next lot.

A couple of days later, Gerry Tunk, Catweazle, Gill (a young Scottish woman from a squat nearby who was very friendly with Catweazle), Russell (who also lived in Gill's squat), Gaffney and I all chipped in to get £20 of smack. Gill and Gerry went off while the rest of us waited downstairs, sitting around where Catweazle's beanbag normally took centre stage right in front of the TV. Within about fifteen minutes the two of them were back with the gear.

We all sat in a circle and Gill went first, helping herself to her share. After she had hit up, it was Gerry's turn and then, progressing clockwise around the circle, it would be mine. Gerry, however, was very squeamish about the injecting process so Gill was going to do the honours and hit him up.

Using the same needle that she had injected herself with, because there was only one, Gill went through the ritual of loading the portion of heroin into the spoon, adding a few drops of lemon juice, and heating the spoon with a cigarette lighter until the contents achieved an injectable consistency. Then the tip of the syringe was put into the spoon and Gill drew back, loading the contents so it was now ready to inject into Gerry.

I am sitting next to Gerry and as I am going to be next, and this will be my first hit, I am watching the proceedings very closely. The next step is to apply the tourniquet and pump up the arm to make it easier to find a vein. When Gerry has done that and Gill thinks she can find and hit a vein she sticks the needle in and draws back. No blood, which means she has not found the vein so she has another go but that is similarly unsuccessful.

Perhaps Gill just wasn't very good at this or maybe she should have done it before she had helped herself to her share of the gear. Either way, she repeated the process several times without success. She was becoming increasingly desperate in her efforts and I could see that she was inserting the needle and manipulating it, fishing around for the vein. I'm watching this action intently and imagining the damage being done as the needle slices around inside Gerry's arm.

Eventually, Gill draws back and there is blood. Hurray, she's found a vein. When I saw the blood I suddenly felt very dry in the mouth and throat. I jumped up and went out to the kitchen to get a drink of water.

The next thing I knew, Larry was getting a bicycle off me as I lay on the floor. There had been a pushbike in the kitchen leaning against the sink and as I've come into the room I've fainted and knocked it over so that it has fallen onto me as I've collapsed onto the floor. I don't know if they didn't hear this in the room next door, or they were just too preoccupied, either way I lay there until Larry found me and helped me up.

I'm not sure how long I was on the floor but it was long enough. After Larry helped me up, I walked back into the lounge room to see what was going on. They were all sitting back or lying around stoned, and all the gear was gone.

Everyone who hit up that day ended up with hep C. Whether one, or some, or all but one were infected on that occasion I guess we will never know. What I do know is that I've always felt like I was saved that day, and I've always been grateful.

Ever since then I've been squeamish about needles and blood. If I see the needle in a doctors' surgery or at the dentist, the needle that will be used on me, I'm likely to go very faint.

Smash and grab

One night after several of us from the squat had been to see a punkish Scottish band called The Fire Engines at a pub in Fulham, we held an informal party back at Pellant Road. I can't recall exactly what I had taken that night but there was certainly quite a bit of alcohol and it seems likely that some other substances were also involved.

For a long time I couldn't make sense of what happened later that night but recently I remembered an important detail and that, I believe, has helped me to understand. The key thing is that I ran into Tim Reece that night at the Fire Engines. We were friendly but the meeting was a little awkward, I guess because we were turning in different circles now. What happened to me that I didn't realise at the time was that the encounter reminded me of my all but forgotten political ideals that had descended into drink and drugs and little else. I was ashamed and embarrassed but I didn't know it and, of course, I responded in a completely irrational way.

A couple of days prior to the post-Fire Engines-party, I had seen a bottle shop on Munster Road that simply had spirits sitting in an unprotected front window. Crucially there was no mesh behind the glass. When the drinks had all but gone at Pellant Road, I suggested going around there and helping ourselves to some of the contents in the window.

Four of us went around there. Along with Gill and I, there were two other people that I did not know or barely knew from the party. When we got around to the bottle shop I simply found a brick and put it straight through the window. My hand was through almost as quickly as the brick. I grabbed a bottle and was off.

This is one of those things where, despite the intoxication, the moment the action was taken it was suddenly revealed for the stupidity that it was, but it was done, and very soon afterwards we could hear the sound of sirens.

There would be no enjoying these ill-gotten fruits that night, nor later. It was now flight and hide. Our plan had not actually extended beyond the point of grabbing the alcohol, and not knowing where to go, I fled circuitously but ended back at the squat. Once I got there I went straight upstairs rather than back down to where the party had been.

There seemed to be several sirens and, given how well some of the inhabitants below were known, it wasn't that long before a police car pulled up out the front and several police went downstairs. I climbed up through the manhole in the ceiling and hid in the roof.

The police didn't stay for long. They left taking Gill with them. After waiting a couple of hours in the roof, I came back down and went to sleep.

At six in the morning another two or more carloads of police turned up. They were asking for Gaffney and I, and as soon as we were identified we were loaded into separate police cars and taken to Fulham Police Station. I don't remember much about the arrest apart from the fact that as I was being loaded into the car one of the police pointed to me and said to another policeman that I was a hard case. I don't know what that remark was based on, possibly just my appearance. I was a bit of a sight because I was thin and pale with a shock of orange hair that was the product of an impatient bleaching exercise.

As soon as we reached the police station I was put into a cell, and told nothing. Each visit to a police cell brought greater claustrophobia and I immediately started doing strenuous exercises. I worked out until I could settle down enough to sit there or lie there without freaking out too much.

Around two hours after I was locked in the cell, the police came and took me away to an interview room. They asked me about my involvement with the smash and grab the previous evening. I denied any knowledge of it. This charade didn't last very long, however, because they pulled out a statement and read it to me. The statement more or less accurately delineated the previous night's action except that it substituted Gaffney for the two others who had been at the party in the squat.

There could be only one source for that statement and that was Gill. She had squealed, identified me, and given Gaffney's name, presumably to defend the other two people involved who must have been friends of hers.

Seeing that the police had a statement and a witness against me I relented. I said Gill and I and two others, definitely not including Gaffney, did it. They pressed me on Gaffney but I was adamant that he was not involved. Then I agreed to make a statement saying that Gill and I and two others unknown to me did it, and that neither of these two was Gaffney who I knew and who was not involved in the burglary.

The police were happy now but I was put back into the cell. I didn't know at the time, but while I was back in the cell the police interviewed Gaffney and then let him go.

Another hour or so later after I had been put back into the cell, a policeman came and got me out. I was escorted again to the same couple of police who read my statement. They said Gaffney should be grateful and then I was bailed to appear in court.

Strangely, after I got back to the squat, Gaffney, Catweazle and Gill and I went and had a very late brunch at a local café. It was a very odd feeling having that meal with Gill at the table, knowing full well that she had to be the one who had dobbed me in.

For me, petty as the whole thing was, these were desperate days. Opinion was mixed on whether I would be sent to prison and the prospect terrified me.

The day of the court case, squat residents who were in the position to know gave me quite a bit of advice on how to proceed and likely outcomes. I recall Frank being especially helpful.

An airline bag was packed with a few clothes and other necessities. I had a small pouch of Old Holborn tobacco, which was my usual smoke at the time. I was advised to squash the tobacco down as tightly as possible and then fluff up the top bit so it looked like I had very little left. This, they said, reduced the chance of the tobacco being taken off me.

Prior to the case I was put into a cell below the court. A court lawyer came along and advised me. Well officially, I suppose, that's what happened. I don't recall him saying anything of any use and I remember being beyond disappointment at the time.

The only favour that Gill did for me in the whole ordeal was to stand beside me in the dock. We just looked like the most hopeless couple.

Interestingly, while Gill's statement was used to have me confess, it was my statement, or what was supposed to be my statement, that was read to the court. I was asked if it was the statement that I had made. I said the statement was similar to the one I had signed in the police station.

On the basis of that statement, Gill was fined and dismissed. I was told to wait while the matter of my previous unpaid fine was considered. Fortunately, in my desperation I had somehow managed to gather the necessary amount. The magistrate then fined me and put me on a good behaviour bond, after which she gave some advice designed to deter me from appearing there again.

A little something to go home on

This conviction was the end of the game for me. I could now see that something that had started out as a more or less spontaneous but politically motivated adventure had degenerated into a one-way trip to gaol, and I definitely did not want to go there. Each time I had been put into the cells had been worse. If you are prone to claustrophobia, a prison cell is not the place to be.

Larry and Gaffney announced that they were going to Greece and asked me if I wanted to go. I was too tired for another expedition and just wanted out. I had no money for myself, let alone to pay the fine and I was never going to make enough to save a fare back to Australia. So, prodigal son-like, I begged my parents for the airfare. Fortunately, they were forthcoming.

They sent me enough for a standard economy fare from London to Australia. I shopped around and found the greatest bargain of all time. Needless to say it was not a direct flight. In fact it was a Philippines Airlines flight that went to Melbourne from London via Frankfurt, Karachi and Bangkok, with a change of planes and an eight-hour wait at Manila.

During the time between my conviction and the flight back to Australia, I had a short and strange relationship with a woman from another nearby squat named Mary. I met her at a local party and then she came back to my room. Mary was a heroin user and she was on the game. I liked her and I needed some emotional support at the time, but what she seemed to want was a pimp. She was keener on me accompanying her as she went to work than she was on sleeping with me. It's possible though that the latter would have followed the former.

The day that I was leaving the squat in Pellant Road several of the people there, including Gerry, Catweazle, Frank and Mary gave me small gifts. It must have been early in Frank's cycle because what I got was several lots of Valium. I was given about a dozen tablets in total, and we are talking about the industrial strength ones. Then I headed off to Heathrow, and Australia, maybe never to return.

For the first few hours of the flight, things went quite well in a boring kind of a way. I had three seats on the side of the plane to myself, as almost everyone did. The plane was about a third full. I idled away those early hours looking out the window watching the map of Europe outside becoming a map of Asia.

You would have to bear in mind the sight I would have been. I am naturally extremely white. One aboriginal bloke that I played football with said I was the whitest white man he had ever seen. I had not exactly been soaking up the sun. I was unhealthy and my shock of semi-curly normally dark brown hair was still mostly orange from the incomplete bleaching exercise.

The one male flight attendant on the plane came along to chat with me. He was nice enough and he managed to find something that we had in common — we had both gone to school in Adelaide — but I felt he was trying to ascertain if I was going to be any trouble. I wasn't planning on being any trouble but, what with one thing and other, it turned out I was.

Not long after our nice friend left, I noticed that the people across the aisle and one row forward were having one glass of champagne after another and they weren't the only ones who seemed to prefer the bubbly. When I asked, they told me that while the beer and spirits had to be paid for the champagne was free. Immediately I ordered a glass of champers. The glass arrived promptly and it was accompanied by a small package of spiced nuts, very nice.

The nuts made a perfect foil for the champagne. I drank the wine and felt like the nuts. I ate the nuts and felt like the wine. And so on. After a few rounds of this I formed the idea that it might be even more pleasant if I had a Valium or two. I ended up having at least a few and then I was extremely comfortable. The last thing I remember seeing out the window was the Indian coast just south of Bangladesh. Then I lay down across all three seats and went to sleep.

I was roused by the sound and the jolt as the wheels hit the tarmac. I looked up and for a moment I struggled to work out where I was. I looked around and saw that I was still lying across the same three seats that I had occupied before I went to sleep but the plane was now completely full. Apart from the two spare ones I was using, I could not see a single vacant seat on the plane.

The scene started to make sense when I realised that we were landing in Manila, not Bangkok as I would have been inclined to think. No one said anything to me but it was obvious that when the aircraft had landed in Bangkok it had taken on hundreds more passengers. Initially, I assumed that the staff had not been able to rouse me as I lay across the spare seats when the plane was in Bangkok. Later I had thought that it might have been even worse. I could have said or done anything when they tried to wake me and get me to sit up and then not been able to remember it. Whatever had happened, the staff had decided it was easier to leave me there asleep and lying across the three seats, presumably while they made alternative arrangements for the passengers who were supposed to occupy those seats.

The plane was emptied in Manila, and those of us going on to other destinations, mainly Australia, were herded into a large corrugated iron shed which contained basic hygiene services and a couple of drink machines. We sat there in the humidity for about eight hours before boarding the next flight. That flight was full and unexceptional and we arrived at Melbourne Airport on time.

I should have expected that I would be given some special treatment when I went through customs and if I had that expectation I wouldn't have been disappointed. When I got to the counter my entire belongings — that is, the backpack, a few clothes and sundries — were all taken out and spread about. Anything that could be disassembled was. There were a few Valium tablets left. As far as they knew I could have gotten them legitimately from any number of doctors in London. In any case, that it is not what they were looking for. After all my effects had been scrutinised, I was taken off to a small white room where I was strip-searched.

I was not surprised at my treatment, I had almost expected it, but I was tired and indignant and when the customs officials finally let me go I asked if they really believed that I would be a drug carrier looking like I was. One member of the staff said I might have brought drugs in for personal use. I responded with a foolish and empty threat, saying that next time I came through customs I would wear a suit and have heroin in my briefcase. Then I headed off to downtown Melbourne.

Knowing Melbourne very poorly as I did, things almost went array there. I found my way to Spencer Street Station and bought a ticket to Adelaide. There were a few hours to play with so I wandered a couple of blocks into the city and adjourned to a quiet little pub. I sat there, idling away the hours, really enjoying myself. I had several beers and watched the scenery.

I liked it so much that I didn't want to rush off to the railway station unnecessarily early. When I did wander off I wasn't exactly sure what direction to go but knew I was just a couple of blocks from the station. Somehow I ended up at the Flinders Street Station with only about five minutes until the train was due to depart from the Spencer Street Station. I had to sprint, as best I could, from one station to the other. I don't know how I managed to catch the train but I did. This time most of the journey was taken up in what might be described as a more legitimate sleep.

Stepping out onto North Terrace in Adelaide the following morning I was shocked by the sparseness of it. The day was pleasant and sunny and the street was wide and tree-lined but there was almost no one there. This was mid-morning on a Saturday. Coming from a couple of years in densely-populated London, the scene was almost shocking and it was actually more like how I had imagined the town from which I originally came.

Then there was nothing else to do but to get a bus to Thebarton where Narelle lived. Narelle was my flame from before my overseas misadventure. I found the address and knocked on the door and there was my old babe. We fell into each other's arms and for me it felt like heaven.

Final chapter

That didn't last long.

Author's note

This book is a work of fiction. With the exception of Margaret Thatcher, Gough Whitlam, Elvis Costello, Siouxsie Sioux, Ian Drury, Lou Reed, etc., all the characters in this book are made up and any resemblance to any person living or dead is coincidental.

www.ingramcontent.com/pod-product-compliance
Lightning Source LLC
Chambersburg PA
CBHW022154260626
47155CB00018B/1873